*LINDA
1996*

THE SAFETY OF HIS ARMS

"I can only thank you for arriving when you did," said Eleanor, raising her eyes, bright with gratitude, toward Andrew's. "It has been so long since I have seen you. What an odious bit of luck that we should at last meet again under such an embarrassing circumstance! Yet, I must say that there is no one else I should rather have come to my rescue. I—I don't know how I may ever show my gratitude!"

Andrew looked down at the young woman he held in his arms and formed a fairly good notion of what form he would like to see her gratitude expressed. "It wasn't luck that brought me to this room. I saw you leave the conservatory with Trowbridge," said Andrew, neatly failing to mention the spark of jealousy that had caused him to go in search of her in the first place. He looked down at her with a suddenly stern expression. "Eleanor, you must not go off alone with a man in future."

"No? Not even if the man is you?"

Andrew's eyes briefly scanned her upturned face as he tightened his arms about her. *"Especially* if the man is me."

Eleanor felt Andrew's arms tighten about her and felt her own heart quicken in response. The movement of his long fingers about her waist and shoulders sent a wave of unfamiliar sensations dancing through her. She felt a little breathless and light-headed as her head tipped back against his shoulder and she gazed up into his face.

Her gaze traveled to his lips. In that moment, she wanted nothing more than for Andrew to kiss her . . .

ZEBRA'S REGENCY ROMANCES DAZZLE AND DELIGHT

A BEGUILING INTRIGUE   (4441, $3.99)
by Olivia Sumner

Pretty as a picture Justine Riggs cared nothing for propriety. She dressed as a boy, sat on her horse like a jockey, and pondered the stars like a scientist. But when she tried to best the handsome Quenton Fletcher, Marquess of Devon, by proving that she was the better equestrian, he would try to prove Justine's antics were pure folly. The game he had in mind was seduction—never imagining that he might lose his heart in the process!

AN INCONVENIENT ENGAGEMENT   (4442, $3.99)
by Joy Reed

Rebecca Wentworth was furious when she saw her betrothed waltzing with another. So she decides to make him jealous by flirting with the handsomest man at the ball, John Collinwood, Earl of Stanford. The "wicked" nobleman knew exactly what the enticing miss was up to—and he was only too happy to play along. But as Rebecca gazed into his magnificent eyes, her errant fiancé was soon utterly forgotten.

SCANDAL'S LADY   (4472, $3.99)
by Mary Kingsley

Cassandra was shocked to learn that the new Earl of Litton was her childhood friend, Nicholas St. John. After years at sea and mixed feelings Nicholas had come home to take the family title. And although Cassandra knew her place as a governess, she could not help the thrill that went through her each time he was near. Nicholas was pleased to find that his old friend Cassandra was his new next door neighbor, but after being near her, he wondered if mere friendship would be enough . . .

HIS LORDSHIP'S REWARD   (4473, $3.99)
by Carola Dunn

As the daughter of a seasoned soldier, Fanny Ingram was accustomed to the vagaries of military life and cared not a whit about matters of rank and social standing. So she certainly never foresaw her *tendre* for handsome Viscount Roworth of Kent with whom she was forced to share lodgings, while he carried out his clandestine activities on behalf of the British Army. And though good sense told Roworth to keep his distance, he couldn't stop from taking Fanny in his arms for a kiss that made all hearts equal!

A SCANDALOUS SEASON

Nancy Lawrence

ZEBRA BOOKS
Kensington Publishing Corp.

http://www.zebrabooks.com

ZEBRA BOOKS are published by

Kensington Publishing Corp.
850 Third Avenue
New York, NY 10022

First Printing: November, 1996
10 9 8 7 6 5 4 3 2 1

Printed in the United States of America

Chapter One

London, 1812

"If I may not marry Charles, I—I shan't marry *anyone!*" Lady Eleanor Chilton exclaimed in a voice of passion.

Lady Glower regarded her niece with a stunned expression. "My dear Eleanor! I am convinced you cannot possibly mean such a thing! Dear Edward," she beseeched as she turned toward her brother, "please tell me that she cannot possibly mean such a thing!"

Lord Dessborough, having witnessed his daughter's dramatic outburst and the tragic manner in which her small, gloved hand fluttered helplessly over her heart, shook his head sadly and said, "Oh, she means it! No doubt of that! Pert, willful—that's Eleanor! And no one but me to blame for indulging her every whim and allowing her to become such a headstrong minx!"

Lady Glower's bewilderment increased. "But—but, it

is every young girl's *dream* to have a London Season! That is why, dearest Eleanor, your papa has brought you here to me in London so you may be presented with my own dear Iris. Don't you think it is most generous of your dear papa?''

"No, I do not!" replied Eleanor, with finality. "A London Season is of all things what I desire least! And I have told Papa so countless times!"

Lady Glower cast her brother a look of reproach. "How is this? Edward, you mentioned nothing of this in your letters to me!"

"Well, I couldn't very well tell you beforehand what kind of maggot has got into her head this time," replied Lord Dessborough, shifting uncomfortably under the weight of his sister's stare. "She's just in one of her moods. It will pass, and then she'll settle down and be a very good sort of girl. Won't you, Minx?"

"I am not in a mood!" said Eleanor, with a hint of defiance. "And I shall never change my mind in this regard. I tell you, I do *not* want to be presented and I do *not* want a London season! Please take me home, Papa! *Please* take me!"

Lord Dessborough resisted her pleas with an obvious effort. "Now, Minx! I'm only trying to do what's best for you," he said, coaxingly. "Your own dear mother wanted you to be presented. Talked about doing the deed herself from the time you were just a little thing. I should think you would want to please your mother's memory and have yourself a season. You'll see! Balls, assemblies, new gowns! Just the sort of thing a young girl like you needs to put her out of a mood!"

Lady Eleanor Chilton's soft, pink lips pursed into a stubborn line of purpose, and her pale blue eyes sparked bright with determination. Her father, usually no match for a will stronger than his own, had proved to be unusually resolute upon the subject of Eleanor's presentation to London society. Thus far, she had tried pleas, feigned illness, and tears in an effort to sabotage his plans to have her presented under her aunt's aegis. Lord Dessborough, however, remained uncharacteristically steadfast.

Since Eleanor's relationship with her father had always been one of affection and trust, she had never needed to learn the finer points of manipulation. Butting heads with her father over an issue was a new and unwelcome experience for her, and she was at a loss to know how to proceed. She decided to try a new tack and leaned over to clasp Lady Glower's hand in a pleading grip. "Dearest aunt! I appeal to you as a woman! Surely you understand how powerful an emotion love can be!"

Lady Glower stiffened visibly. "Love? Whatever do you mean, Eleanor?"

"Oh, she has it in her head that she's in love," interpolated Lord Dessborough. "Seems she's pledged herself to the Adair boy. You know! He's the son of the squire on the estate that neighbors Dessborough Place to the north. Likeable lad, but no bronze. Eleanor can do better!"

"But I don't *want* to do better," exclaimed Eleanor before she could stop herself. "That is—Charles Adair will make a splendid husband and—and I love him!"

Lady Glower fixed her brother with a glare that promised to bore two holes right through the middle of his forehead. "Edward! This situation is beyond all! You mentioned nothing of such an attachment in any of your letters! If Eleanor has, indeed, formed a *tendre* for this young man—"

"No, no! Nothing of the like, you can be sure," said Lord Dessborough, quickly. "Why, Eleanor and Charles have known each other since their cradle days. They're playmates, that's all! This marriage business of theirs is nothing but a fancy! One of their games! I'm sure I never heard of their making a match of it until we were packed and ready to board the chaise for London. Pay her no heed!"

"But I *love* him!" Eleanor exclaimed, making a great effort to produce a tear that might at last prove her sincerity.

Lord Dessborough anxiously observed her efforts. "Dash it, Eleanor! None of that, now! From the day I first proposed bringing you to your Aunt Glower in London, you've blown in one storm after another. I'm beginning to think you're composed almost entirely of water! Why, this ain't like you at all! My Eleanor would never throw her heart over! Game as a pebble with plenty of bottom—that's the Eleanor I know!"

"Edward, she is not a racehorse!" said Lady Glower sternly. Producing a delicate lace kerchief as if by magic, she handed it to Eleanor, then took a seat beside her niece on the small settee and wrapped a supportive arm about her slim shoulders. "You cannot merely aim this poor girl at a fence and expect her to jump! Eleanor has feelings and desires of her own. Perhaps the timing is not right for her to be presented. Perhaps she should wait until next year to make her curtsies in the Queen's drawing room."

Eleanor rewarded her aunt's kindness with a misty-eyed smile that she hoped would encourage Lady Glower to defend her more in the future.

Lord Dessborough, however, was not convinced. "Wait another year? Dash it, the girl's already on the shady side of nineteen! We must do the deed this year or never."

"Never!" said Eleanor, briefly emerging from behind the kerchief into which she had been making a great show of emotion.

"Edward, I won't have you distressing Eleanor so!" Lady Glower scolded. "Is it any wonder the dear girl hasn't been herself? The poor motherless child! At this time in her life she needs a woman's guidance and—"

"Devil take it, of course she needs a woman's guidance!" exclaimed Lord Dessborough with a sudden and uncommon flash. "That's why I brought her to you! She can't continue on as she has been with only me to guide her footsteps—for I'm no guidance at all! It's been my way to give her her head and let her run. Thankfully, she's a sensible girl and she's done all right by herself, learning the things girls are supposed to learn. But now—well, the thing is, I haven't made any effort at all to see that Eleanor was raised according to her mother's wishes. When I think about it, I feel downright guilty. Thankfully, I don't think about it often and it's too late now anyway—except for this curtsey business! Eleanor's mother was quite keen on the idea. Talked about it all the time! And it's my belief that if I do nothing else, I should make sure I do the one thing she had her heart set on. Eleanor's mother wanted her presented, and I'm here to see that it happens."

Eleanor emerged once again from behind the kerchief, a rebuke at the ready, but her father cut her off, saying, "There's no use arguing, for my mind is made up. Eleanor, you know I've never turned Turkish with you before, but in this instance I won't be dissuaded! You shall stay here in London with your aunt and be presented along with your cousin. There!"

Eleanor recognized a note of conviction to her father's words that persuaded her that further argument would prove useless. "Very well," she said, sadly. "I shall stay and be presented with my cousin, Iris. But I shan't enjoy myself and I shall pine every day for Charles!"

"There's a girl!" commended Lord Dessborough, satisfied. "If you're going to wallow in misery, you might just as well do it in a ballroom with music to accompany you!"

"Papa," said Eleanor, suddenly thoughtful, "is it true what you said? *Did* Mama particularly desire that I should be presented? *Did* she want me to have a Season?"

He looked at her with some surprise. "I've never stained false with you before, have I?"

"No, Papa. But you rarely speak of Mama and I certainly have no memory of her. It is rather curious, I think, that my come-out should have meant so much to her."

"Oh, not at all!" said Lady Glower. "You see, your mama often referred to her London Season as one of the happiest times of her life! It was then, after all, that she met your papa!"

With a slight effort, Lord Dessborough conjured up a long-forgotten memory. "Bless me, what a beauty she was! Had more beaux about her than she knew what to do with! Brought us all to heel in short order, I can tell you!"

"How like her you are, my dear Eleanor," Lady Glower said, clasping her niece's hand in an affectionate squeeze. "You have your mother's looks, you know. She was also very delicate with her blond hair and blue eyes. Sometimes when I look at you, I'm quite taken by your resemblance to the dear woman."

Lord Dessborough trailed a gentle finger down his daughter's cheek. "I'll wager you never thought of yourself as a beauty before, eh, Minx? Only wait until your Aunt Glower has finished with you. You'll be a belle among belles this season!"

"There is no time to waste," said Lady Glower purposefully. "We must begin shopping immediately if we are to have her gowns ready in time for the first ball of the season."

Her brother gave her an encouraging nod. "Rig her out right and send the nonsense to me!"

"You may rely upon it! Your Eleanor and my Iris shall have a splendid season!"

"Capital!" said Lord Dessborough. He stood by the fireplace and beamed down upon them with a smile of great satisfaction.

Eleanor, however, was not quite as pleased. She had been listening to her aunt and father with mixed emotions. If forced, she would have had to admit that the prospect of a London season was a rather dazzling one. Under any other circumstance, she was sure she would have enjoyed all the various entertainments to be offered up; but her heart was engaged and her hand was pledged to Charles Adair long before she ever boarded her father's chaise for London.

If her father was set upon seeing her presented in order to fulfill her mother's dying wish, Eleanor would not deny him; but if his hopes were planted in Eleanor's contracting a marriage proposal during her stay, she knew she was destined to disappoint him.

She felt it prudent to make one final push to ensure that her father and aunt understand her situation perfectly, and said in a firm voice, "If your idea of a successful season is to see me engaged to anyone but Charles, I beg you will not put yourself to the trouble of presenting me! Papa, I have no choice but to do as you ask and make my curtsey to the Queen. And I shall attend all the balls and routs and drums you desire, but—but I shall never enjoy myself!"

The drawing room door opened during this speech and Lady Glower's daughter entered the room. Miss Iris Glower was eighteen years old, but a pair of large, innocent brown eyes coupled with a disposition that was rather shy in company, made her appear younger.

She favored her uncle with a quick curtsey and then hurried to Eleanor's side, exclaiming, "Cousin! I just received word that you had arrived! How famous to have you here in London with us! But what odd things you do say! Never enjoy yourself at a ball? What can you mean?"

The startling possibility that Eleanor's reluctance to be presented might have an influence on a girl as impressionable as Iris was a factor Lady Glower had not before considered. She said with an uneasy laugh, "Inquisitive girl! You ask far too many questions, Iris dear. Your cousin was merely being modest. Of course she must enjoy herself!"

Iris's eyes reflected the curiosity of a multitude of unasked questions, but she recognized the warning tone in her mother's voice and didn't press her cousin for details until they had bade a fond farewell to Lord Dessborough and were at last alone in Eleanor's bedroom.

"You are very brave, Cousin, to defy your papa and my mama in that way," said Iris, admiringly.

Eleanor knew a momentary pang of guilt. "But I don't mean to be defiant, truly! I only wish to marry Charles Adair, but I cannot convince my papa that no one else shall suit me!"

"Perhaps your sentiments may change," ventured Iris. "Perhaps you shall attend a *ton* party and gain the notice of some fabulously eligible gentleman."

Eleanor gave her blond curls a slight shake. "I could never entertain such an offer, no matter how flattering. Charles is the only man for whom I shall ever feel any degree of attachment."

Iris sighed deeply. "How very romantic! Is he passionately in love with you? I suppose he has nursed a deep affection for you all these years, but was never able to speak because he was overcome by your beauty!"

Eleanor laughed. "Oh, pooh!"

"Tell me about him. Is he rich? Is he handsome?"

"I suppose he is handsome," said Eleanor after a thoughtful moment. "As for his wealth, I do not believe his pockets are too deep, but his family lives quite comfortably."

These remarks made Iris stare. "You don't at all sound like a woman in love," she said, accusingly. "There is no dreamy look in your eyes when his name is mentioned, and you don't swoon at the mere thought of seeing him once again."

"You'll find such behavior only between the pages of a novel from the lending library," said Eleanor, with authority. "Charles and I were friends long before we ever decided we should marry. We deal very comfortably together."

"If that is your feeling, I cannot help but wonder that you might meet someone you shall like better," said Iris, reasonably.

Eleanor's blond curls danced once again with a fierce shake of her head. "Impossible! Charles and I are destined to marry! Oh, I know you are much disappointed that ours is not a torrid passion, but I *do* love Charles after a fashion. I think I should like very much to be his wife. We are pledged, you know, and we are in the habit of spending a good deal of time together every day. I think he was quite overcome that I should have to leave him to come to London, and I'm very much concerned that he shall pine and waste away without me."

"How horrid!" exclaimed Iris, thinking that this, at last, sounded like the actions of a person in love.

"Yes, indeed! So I have charged my dearest friend, Georgianna Turpin, with tending him and making sure that he does not fall into a complete melancholy. I know Georgianna shall do her best by him. She's a very compliant girl, with the sweetest of dispositions." Eleanor laughed slightly and said, "She's not at all like me!"

"She sounds quite missish," said Iris, scornfully.

"Oh, she's very dear, and Charles likes her. I think they shall deal extremely well together while I am gone. I mean to return to them as quickly as possible—Just as soon as I can convince your mama that she is making a great waste of her time by presenting me and squiring me about town."

Iris looked worried. "But Mama has made great plans, you know. She has already accepted several invitations for us, and there is to be a ball here at Glower House in less than a month's time!"

"By then I shall be back at home, spending my days with Charles," said Eleanor, with a martial set to her chin.

Iris regarded her with wonder. "What a curious girl you are, Cousin. Imagine! Not wanting to wear new gowns and flirt with attentive men and dance the night away! I'm sure I never before heard a young lady speak as you do!"

"Oh, I have no doubt of that!" said Eleanor, ingenuously. "My papa says I am much too headstrong and willful, but, of course, there is nothing to be done about it now for I am quite set in my ways. I know I'm not like the other girls who will be making their curtsies, for I can hardly be described as fresh out of the schoolroom, on the scramble and anxious to set up her home. I already help manage Papa's estates, keep his house, and act as his hostess; and I'm quite accustomed to making my own decisions." She turned upon Iris with a pointed look. "Haven't *you* ever wanted to make decisions for yourself, Cousin?"

"I—I never considered such a thing," said Iris, a good deal surprised. "If I were to behave as you do, I don't know *what* Mama would say!"

Eleanor laughed. "Oh, I think I can guess! But remember that I am not at all like you, Cousin! I am quite well used to handling Papa, and I think I shall very quickly convince your mama that it would be best for all concerned if she were to send me home straight away. If my plan works, I might contrive to be home in a fortnight.''

From past experience, Iris Glower knew better than to doubt her cousin when she spoke in just that tone. Eleanor Chilton was determined and willful, but then again, the same might be said of Lady Glower. If Eleanor were resolved to leave London, she would no doubt find Lady Glower to be just as resolved that she stay. Iris knew a nagging feeling that in this regard, dear, determined Cousin Eleanor might at last have met her match.

Chapter Two

"Eleanor, how *could* you?" Iris hissed into her cousin's ear above the din of the crowded ballroom. "Refusing to be partnered for dance after dance—and with the most eligible of men! I swear, Eleanor, you have more brass!"

Eleanor turned toward Iris with a look of exaggerated innocence. "But I thought to have been all politeness! I did, after all, decline to dance with thanks!"

"That is hardly the point," said Iris, worriedly. "I don't know what Mama shall say. I'm convinced she shall be quite furious with you!"

As they had so many times in the two weeks since her arrival, Eleanor's blue eyes sparked with defiance and she mutinously lifted her chin. She gazed out upon the crowded ballroom of their hostess, Lady Harpole, with a schooled expression of impassivity, determined to repel with a single look any man with thoughts of partnering her in a dance. "I am here against my will," she said, in Gothic accents, "and I have already told your mama many times that I shall never enjoy myself!"

"But—but couldn't you *never* enjoy yourself while you dance?" asked Iris, fretfully.

Eleanor turned upon her with a look of injured betrayal. "How can you say such a thing? I thought you, if anyone, would be sympathetic to my situation!"

"Oh, but I am sympathetic!" Iris assured her quickly. "It's all so romantic! Your devotion to Charles is just as it should be, but—but, you've been quite cold and reserved at every function we have thus far attended. If you aren't careful, dear Cousin, you shall earn a shocking reputation!"

"Good!" replied Eleanor, once again training her arctic gaze upon the dancers. "Then, perhaps, I shall be quite ruined and Aunt shall send me home in disgrace. Then at last Charles and I may be together. Yes, I believe a shocking reputation may prove to be the very thing!"

She was well on her way toward getting her wish. The season was young and London was still rather thin of company; yet Eleanor had already accompanied her aunt and cousin to several at-homes, two musical soirees, and one assembly at Almack's rooms where she was introduced to any number of young people and several eligible bachelors, in particular. To each she had addressed some very civil remark when required, but her manner had been cool, her lovely countenance austere; and she had discovered, quite by chance, that such a bloodless, icy demeanor had the power to repel potential suitors as nothing else could.

At last Eleanor believed that she had hit upon a device that should place her so far removed from Lady Glower's good graces, that she should be sent back to the country, posthaste. She failed, however, to consider Society's capriciousness.

A chance remark by a leading dowager had already convinced Lady Glower that Eleanor's reserve was somehow attractive; and upon their visit to Almack's, one of that establishment's more forbidding patronesses had taken great care to express to Lady Glower the opinion that Lady Eleanor Chilton was a girl worthy of admiration. "Such a lovely child! A beauty, and so well behaved! Not the least sign of putting herself forward! With every young miss in town set and determined to gain attention, it is most refreshing to see your niece conduct herself with propriety!"

Nothing more was required to convince Lady Glower that Eleanor should be allowed to freeze like a block of ice whenever she stepped across the threshold of a ballroom, if she so desired.

Eleanor, unaware that her behavior had already become one of the more often discussed *on-dits* of the young season, continued to do her best to repel the romantic notions of as many young men of her circle as she thought possible.

She was thus engaged, gazing dispassionately about the perimeter of Lady Harpole's ballroom from her place near dowager's row, when she saw two gentlemen enter the room through the far doors. They were both tall men, which accounted for their initially having caught her attention. What kept her attention she could not readily say.

One of the men was dressed in military garb. His manner was dashing, his coloring fair, and he was smiling in obvious enjoyment of his surroundings.

His companion was slightly taller with dark hair and

eyes, and he was dressed in a manner that Eleanor had never before encountered. Until that moment, she had thought that there were a number of very fashionable gentlemen present. With their high-point collars, extravagant waistcoats, and dazzling rings and watch fobs, they had reminded her of dear Charles Adair and how she had always considered him to be the handsomest man of her acquaintance.

The tall gentleman standing in the doorway wrought serious injury to that notion. He stood in perfect contrast to the lavish dress of Charles Adair and all the dandies milling about the ballroom. His coat and pantaloons were black and followed the lines of his broad shoulders and manly figure without the need for padding or cinching; his waistcoat was purest white, above which fell the delicate folds of his white cravat. Eleanor found the effect of this quiet, masterly style to be quite stunning.

His companion spoke to him and laughed, but the tall gentleman's dark eyes continued to scan the ballroom with an expression of indifference that put to shame Eleanor's own look of practiced tedium. When his dark eyes suddenly met her wide blue ones, she realized that she had been staring, and she felt an unwelcome blush mantle her cheeks as she yanked her gaze from his.

Eleanor forced herself to survey the ballroom with deliberate calm before she allowed herself to look at the tall man again with what she hoped was a casual air. Then she discovered that he had leveled his quizzing glass at her. A sudden wave of outrage and unfamiliar confusion swept over her, but she was determined to maintain her hard-won reputation and struck a frigid pose.

"Eleanor! There is a very bold sort of man staring at you!" hissed Iris.

Eleanor's chin went up a notch. "Really? I hope I shall not be compelled to make the acquaintance of such a dismally rude person!"

"He's very handsome," said Iris, helpfully. "I don't believe I have ever seen a finer gentleman!"

"That is no gentleman," countered Eleanor, still keenly aware of his scrutiny. She could not quite prevent herself from asking, "I don't suppose you may know his name?"

"No, but Mama shall introduce us if she thinks him a proper sort. I do hope she does not, for I truly don't know what I should say to such a man!"

Eleanor was inclined to share her cousin's opinion, but thought better than to say so.

Curiosity drew her gaze once again toward the doorway a mere moment later, and an odd rush of disappointment swept over her when she realized that the two tall gentlemen were no longer there.

Lady Glower came upon Eleanor and Iris in a rush, exclaiming, "At last I've found you! You shall never guess, my dears, who has arrived, but Sir Andrew de Ardescote! He is on the arm of Captain Lisle—who is dear Lady Harpole's nephew—and I am *assured* Lady Harpole will introduce you! My dears, I hardly know what to think!"

Iris shifted nervously. "Sir Andrew? Here? Oh, Mama, whatever shall I say to him?"

"You must let him speak first, my dear, and then you

have only to follow his lead. Now do stop frowning in that worried way and do try to look pleased!''

"*Who* is Sir Andrew de Ardescote?'' asked Eleanor, unsure whether to be alarmed or intrigued.

"Of course you are not yet familiar with our leaders of society, being just in town from the country,'' said Lady Glower generously, "but it is past time you learned, my dear! *Everyone* follows Sir Andrew's lead! He is known as The Fashionable Corinthian, and I assure you, no one person's opinion counts for more! There's his fortune, of course, and the fact that he is related to the first one hundred families, besides being the grandson of a marquess. Add to that his intimate friendship with the Prince of Wales, and you have a man who is surely the most eligible catch in the kingdom! If he will speak with you for but a moment, your success shall be assured!'' Lady Glower gave a sudden gasp. "Gracious, here they come!''

Curiosity caused Eleanor to turn and follow the direction of her aunt's gaze. She had never before met such a pattern card of perfection as her aunt had just described, and she spent a good moment peering about the crowded ballroom, vainly seeking a glimpse of that paragon. No such creature appeared before her. Instead, she had a very clear view of the tall gentleman who had peered at her through his quizzing glass from across the room, and she realized that he and his companion were making their way purposefully toward her in Lady Harpole's wake.

Lady Glower smiled benevolently as her good friend, Lady Harpole performed the necessary introductions. From her demeanor it was apparent that Lady Glower set great store in making her daughter and niece known to the two men, for she could barely contain her excitement. Her eyes were bright, her smile tremulous, and her hand, clutching a stylishly painted fan in a deathly grip, trembled ever so slightly as her charges were introduced to Sir Andrew de Ardescote and his friend, Captain Geoffrey Lisle.

Eleanor cast Sir Andrew an appraising look. Here was opportunity indeed! The chance to snub an arbiter of fashion did not come along every day, and Eleanor reasoned that if gaining Sir Andrew's approval meant social success, then earning his censure would certainly bring about her social ruin.

As she watched her aunt move away on Lady Harpole's arm, Eleanor noticed that other nearby guests were now regarding her and Iris with interest. Apparently, Lady Glower had not overrated Sir Andrew's influence. Here certainly was a man whose displeasure must be cultivated. If he took her in dislike, all chances for Eleanor's social success would be reduced to shreds and Lady Glower would have no choice but to arrange her niece's fare back to Dessborough Place.

Iris had responded to Lady Harpole's introductions with her usual blush as she dipped a small, nervous curtsey. Eleanor, made of much sterner stuff, merely nodded her head toward Sir Andrew and asked, with schooled composure, "How do you do?" She was immediately rewarded with the sight of Sir Andrew de Ardescote once again surveying her through his glass.

He noted that Eleanor's reaction was very much as it had been when he had watched her earlier from the other side of the ballroom. Almost he had convinced himself that he must have been mistaken; that some trick of light or reflection had him believing that the lovely Lady Eleanor Chilton had met his scrutiny with a decidedly rebellious response. He now knew that he had not been mistaken, for he found that he was being surveyed in a manner quite as critical as his own. He was not in the habit of seeing a beautiful, well-bred young lady regard him down the length of her delicate nose, and his attention was arrested. When his gaze met hers, he discovered that this particular young lady possessed a decidedly militant spark within the depths of her lovely blue eyes.

He captured her hand and fleetingly brought the tips of her fingers to his lips; then he said with practiced charm, "I do very well, now that I have made your delightful acquaintance."

It was a speech he had delivered on many occasions. Designed to reduce even the most steadfast feminine heart to a simpering, blushing jelly, his mildly flirtatious style had never failed before. But he was fast learning that Lady Eleanor Chilton was not quite in the common way.

Eleanor snatched her hand from his grasp with lightning speed and set her back in a rigid line. She was a young woman whose hand had been kissed many times. A chaste peck and a slight pressure on her fingertips and the thing was done. But some unknown feeling fluttered within her as she felt the brief touch of Sir Andrew's warm breath upon her wrist, and she could only hope that no one else noticed the slight tremble that shook her hand as she offered it in turn to Captain Lisle.

The Captain smiled good-naturedly as he sketched a graceful bow. "Very happy to make your acquaintance at last, ladies! My aunt, Lady Harpole, has spoken of you many times and particularly charged me with making you welcome. My aunt and Lady Glower are great friends, you know! Aunt read me a Methodist's sermon for arriving so late, I can tell you! But our tardiness must be placed at Andrew's door for I had to fairly drag him here. Not one for come-out balls, that's Andrew!''

This ingenuous speech sent Eleanor's delicate eyebrows deliberately flying. Now or never was the time to set her plan in motion and she said in a challenging tone, "Indeed? Then we must be flattered and gratified that you would grace us with your presence!"

Captain Lisle appeared surprised, never having imagined that his artless words might cause offense. He rolled an uncomfortable glance toward his friend, but Sir Andrew was looking only at Eleanor.

He wasn't quite sure whether he was intrigued or nettled by the young lady's uncommonly chilly behavior, but his interest was certainly aroused. Andrew was generally used to being introduced to girls fresh from the schoolroom and seeing them deport themselves in the same mincing and blushing manner as had Miss Iris Glower. Most young ladies hadn't the courage to meet his eye. He saw that Lady Eleanor Chilton had not only the pluck to look fully up into his face, but she did so with a decidedly challenging gleam to her blue eyes.

He wasn't sure what game she was playing, but his attention was caught and he found himself more than willing to play along. He said, "I feel sure you overrate my influence, ma'am."

"Perhaps," said Eleanor, setting her fan into motion with a practiced hand, "but if you do not enjoy a ball such as this, pray do not feel you must delay your departure merely because you have made *our* acquaintance."

Eleanor heard Iris faintly gasp beside her and she saw Sir Andrew blink twice, and she wondered, for the briefest moment, if she had gone too far.

Sir Andrew was wondering very much the same thing. He wasn't accustomed to being ejected from Society's ballrooms by an unknown miss who, for some reason not yet fathomed, had set herself up as his nemesis. His curiosity, rarely piqued, was now careening full force and he knew a sudden desire to discover what, if anything, lay behind her odd manners.

He looked down upon her from his great height and said, with practiced civility, "You mistake, ma'am. I am often known to enjoy a ball or assembly, if I am with those whose company I enjoy."

"Perhaps we should enjoy ourselves more if we were to dance," said Captain Lisle, brightly stepping into the rift. "No sense standing about at a ball. Miss Glower, may I have the honor?" He bowed low before he claimed Iris's hand and led her onto the dance floor.

Eleanor watched them take their places in a set that was forming, and wrestled with her fast-fleeing courage. Hatching a plot that would mastermind her social ruin had seemed a rather safe venture a mere moment before. But incivility was not in her nature, and she was having great difficulty in maintaining a frigid pose in the face of Sir Andrew's charm.

She chanced a look at him and saw that he was watching her, a glimmer of amusement enlivening his dark features.

He bowed slightly and offered his arm, clearly intent on leading her out onto the dance floor. From the placid expression on his face, it was apparent that he expected Eleanor to meekly join him in the set.

Now or never was the time for Eleanor to ensure that her budding social career withered on the vine. She rallied what was left of her courage. Still, she could not quite bring herself to look up into his face as she said, "I assure you, sir, I have not the least intention of dancing. I do hope Lady Harpole did not make me known to you with the promise that I should be your partner."

He was silent beside her and she chanced a look at him. The faint trace of amusement was gone from his expression and he was staring down at her with a darkling look. She thought for a moment that he might rail against her, but his expression went rigid and he merely nodded his head as he said tightly, "As you wish, ma'am."

Eleanor wondered if his anger would cause him to stalk away, leaving her alone and disgraced on the edge of the dance floor. She hardly expected him to remain at her side, but apparently he had every intention of doing just so. He stood so close beside her that Eleanor could sense his tall, muscular body drawing stiff with disapproval. As the uneasy silence between them stretched interminably, she felt a telltale warmth mantle her cheeks. Almost did she beg his pardon; almost did she blurt out the reason for her uncommon, rude behavior; but even as she struggled with these thoughts, the dance ended and Captain Lisle and Iris returned.

As she approached, Iris regarded her cousin with an expressive mixture of anguish and accusation, for she had a rather good idea why Eleanor and Sir Andrew hadn't joined the set.

Captain Lisle, however, blundered innocently upon them. "I swear, Drew, you are a monstrous guest! Here you stand with the loveliest of creatures, and you haven't the good grace to stand up with her in a simple country dance!''

His voice had been teasing, his smile good-natured, but his features underwent a rapid change when he encountered his friend's suddenly stormy expression.

"Lady Eleanor does not dance," replied Sir Andrew in a voice of tight control. "It is, of course, my loss! Perhaps I shall have the pleasure another time." He claimed Eleanor's hand and again brought it to his lips with a bit less dash than he had before. Without another word, he bowed toward Iris and moved away, leaving Captain Lisle no choice but to make his hasty goodbyes and follow in his wake.

Iris barely waited until the two gentlemen were out of earshot before she leveled an accusing look at her cousin. "Eleanor, how *could* you? Refusing to dance with Sir Andrew de Ardescote? I tremble to think what the consequences shall be!"

Eleanor had already embarked upon some trembling of her own. An unexpected feeling of regret swept over her as she recalled the manner in which she had met Sir Andrew's charm with wretched incivility. She suffered the odd notion that she was being watched; that other guests had witnessed her encounter with Sir Andrew and had seen his usually bland expression change to one of surprise before he had gone white with fury after a mere moment in her presence. A hot flush of shame mantled her cheeks as she recalled how Sir Andrew had treated her with impeccable civility even after she had snubbed him. Her plan to be sent home in disgrace suddenly lost a good deal of its appeal.

Eleanor tried to summon a bit of that militant pluck that had served her so well earlier in the evening. Her chin went up as she gazed out across the dance floor, but her expression was more distressed than dispassionate. Her attempt to conjure a mental picture of dear Charles Adair waiting patiently for her return went unrewarded. Instead, before her swam a vision of Sir Andrew's face, looking like the very devil with eyes glinting in sudden anger; and she fervently hoped, with all her being, that she would never have to face Sir Andrew de Ardescote again.

Chapter Three

Sir Andrew de Ardescote glanced about the faro table and said in a languid tone, "Stakes, gentlemen."

Captain Lisle glanced sharply at his friend. There was a glittering hardness to Andrew's eyes that warned him that Andrew was in a foul mood. Add to that the fact that in the short time since they had removed from Lady Harpole's ballroom to White's Andrew had consumed a bottle of the club's best brandy, and Captain Lisle was certain that Andrew's temper was simmering toward an explosion.

Andrew in anger was never a sight he cared to witness, and he wondered, not for the first time that evening, what the ballroom chit could possibly have said to have set his friend off so.

They had left Lady Harpole's house as soon as Captain Lisle had finished dancing with Iris Glower. Andrew had made his goodbyes to his hostess with the polish for which he was famed, but as soon as he had quit the house, his handsome face had turned to a mask of fury. He had set off for White's on foot and Captain Lisle, fearful that his friend's uncommon anger might compel him to do or say something he must later be forced to regret, accompanied him in wary silence.

The faro room at White's had been noisy and crowded when they first arrived, but was now rather thin of company. Andrew had held the bank for the last full hour. His stakes were so high, his manner so ruthlessly unconcerned, that only a sprinkling of the club's most deep-pocketed members remained.

The gentlemen surrounding the faro table placed their bets. Andrew dealt the first card, a queen, and set it down on the table.

"Devil take it!" exclaimed Lord Montfort in a wine-thickened voice as he watched his sizeable wager being swept off the table. "To be scorched by a lady twice in one night! There's a limit to what a man can take, I tell you!"

Andrew raised a dark, sardonic brow as he surveyed Lord Montfort's flushed countenance. "I see your legendary grace is on full display tonight, Monty," he said darkly as he turned up the next card.

The other gentlemen at the table smiled.

"That's Monty, right and tight!" said young Lord Trowbridge. "He's a passion for the ladies and a passion for cards."

"A pity those passions are coupled with the most abominable luck!" said Mr. Tilney, and the gentlemen standing at the faro table erupted in laughter.

A dull flush again swept over Lord Montfort's face. He had been drinking steadily since his arrival. His eyes glittered in the candlelight of the room and his words, when he spoke, were decidedly slurred. "You'd be wise to see to your own luck, Tilney!"

"What's tweaked you this time, Monty?" Captain Lisle asked as he watched Andrew deal the next turn.

"No doubt it was a woman," said Mr. Tilney, knowingly.

Lord Trowbridge shook his head. "Not even a woman! She was little more than a come-out chit! They say she's been on the town less than a month with nothing to recommend her. So what must she do but snub poor Montfort beyond all possibility of recovery!"

"Oh, I must disagree, for I was there to see it happen," Mr. Tilney said, placing his bet for the next turn of the cards. His expression softened at the memory. "In my opinion, the lady did indeed have something to recommend her. She had the face of an angel and a figure just as lovely."

Andrew's strong hand paused a moment in the middle of a deal, but his tone was casual as he said, "And are we to understand that you took exception to such charms, Monty?"

"No, no! The lady took exception to Monty!" said Lord Trowbridge, helpfully.

Lord Montfort's face colored to an alarming degree. "Keep your tongue still, damn you! Is the entire city to know my business?"

"Now, don't take a pet, Monty!" said Lord Trowbridge. "You aren't to be blamed. We know how females are, after all!" He confidently placed his markers on the table for the next turn, and said, "This girl refused to stand up with Monty for a simple country dance! Looked him straight in the eye just as cool as you please and refused him!"

Andrew recognized a certain familiarity with the scene Lord Trowbridge had just described. He frowned slightly but his voice betrayed no emotion as he asked, "And where was this crushing setdown delivered?"

"Lady Harpole's. Well, *you* must have been there! The woman's your aunt, ain't she, Lisle? What does she mean by including such a haughty little chit among her guest list?"

The Captain quickly disclaimed any responsibility for his aunt's affairs. "After all, *I'm* never consulted in these matters!"

Mr. Tilney shook his head thoughtfully. "Doesn't make sense. Monty's eligible enough. Think, man! You must have done something to set the girl's back up."

"More likely," said Lord Trowbridge in a goading tone, "she refused Montfort because she was waiting for de Ardescote to partner her."

Andrew tensed but continued to deal out the cards in a deceptively casual manner that prompted Captain Lisle to shift uncomfortably.

"Here now! You can't lay the blame at Andrew's door because some silly girl cut Montfort!" protested the Captain.

"It's happened before," insisted Lord Trowbridge. "Every toadeater and green girl fresh on the Town tries by trick or trap to catch Andrew's eye. He may have his pick of them! And why? Because they hope he will bring them into fashion! I should think it a curst nuisance, de Ardescote! How do you bear such nonsense?"

He usually bore it very well, for he had long ago accepted the fact that with his reputation as the Fashionable Corinthian came responsibility and a certain amount of inconvenience. But in one fell swoop, a lovely-looking girl with startling blue eyes and hair the color of spun gold had wrought serious injury to his consequence.

As a favor to Lisle and his aunt, Andrew had greeted Lady Eleanor Chilton with the same polished address he usually reserved for his intimates. He had even attempted to engage her in conversation, secure in the knowledge that she would appreciate the fact that such favors were not dispensed every day. Not only had the little baggage been far from grateful for the honor bestowed upon her, she had even taken him to task for arriving late.

This he might have forgiven as nothing more than the peculiar effrontery of a country-bred girl who lacked polish. What he could not forgive was the fact that she had held him up to ridicule. The entire assembly had seen him bow and offer his escort onto the dance floor. The entire assembly had seen her refuse to take his arm.

She had made him look ridiculous, and that in itself was something he could not forgive. But now he was given to understand that she had treated Lord Montfort in the same high-handed manner. The knowledge that a dab of a girl, with nothing to recommend her but her looks, should lump Sir Andrew de Ardescote, the Fashionable Corinthian, with the likes of the ill-mannered, questionably bred Lord Montfort was enough to send his temper to boiling. It was taking quite a bit of effort on his part to project an image of outward calm when simmering just beneath the surface of his composed expression was a strong desire to teach Lady Eleanor Chilton a lesson she would not soon forget.

He dealt the next pair of cards as Lord Montfort

sputtered in impotent anger. "It wasn't any of *my* doing!" he insisted. "The girl must be all about in her head to attend a lavish ball only to refuse dance after dance!"

Andrew's dark brow cocked at a vaguely interested angle. "She danced with no one?"

"Not a soul," confirmed Mr. Tilney with a shake of his head. "The girl stayed the entire night right beside the greenery Lady Harpole had set in one corner of the ballroom."

"Is that so?" asked Andrew, his eyes once again on the cards. "You should have been a potted palm, Monty. At least then the lady might have spent the evening with you."

The other gentlemen at the table laughed, and Lord Montfort colored alarmingly.

Andrew crooked a finger and brought an attending waiter to his side with another bottle of brandy. He drained his glass and allowed the waiter to refill it. Another slight gesture, and the waiter poured fresh brandy into Lord Montfort's glass, as well.

"Do let me fill your glass, Monty," said Andrew, appeasingly. "If I must have your money tonight, it is only right that you must have some of my wine."

Lord Montfort could not bring himself to refuse the brandy, even though Andrew's words rankled. He glared at him and said, rather belligerently, "You have a damned unpleasant tongue, de Ardescote!"

"True," Andrew replied in an unconcerned tone that was only enhanced by the consumption of a considerable amount of excellent liquor, "but I shouldn't try to curb it, if I were you."

Lord Montfort had no intention of making such an

attempt. His brain might be clouded with brandy fumes and his common sense at risk, but he was well aware that beneath Sir Andrew's exquisitely tailored veneer was a man generally accorded to be one of the best shots in England and a pugilist renowned for being handy with his fives. The notion occurred to Lord Montfort through a swimming head that Sir Andrew's manner was a bit more reckless, more challenging than usual, and that he seemed to be spoiling for a fight. A brief moment of reflection convinced him that locking horns with an inebriated Sir Andrew de Ardescote was undoubtedly a more dangerous prospect than he was prepared to face. He decided against making any retort for the more fulfilling prospect of tossing the brandy in his glass back in one gulp.

A moment of uncomfortable silence followed until Mr. Tilney stepped into the breach, saying in a falsely bright voice, "Thank the gods that's settled! I never thought I should see such a dust kicked up over a come-out chit! Lisle, you've some answering to do for this one!"

Captain Lisle was immediately defensive. "Here now, I told you it has nothing to do with me! My Aunt Harpole invited the girl as a favor to her friend, Lady Glower! It was all their doing! You can't lay the business at *my* door!"

"Who was she anyway?" asked Lord Trowbridge, searching his hazy memory. "I know I was introduced to the girl, but damme if I can recall her name!"

"Her name is Chilton," said Captain Lisle, helpfully. "Lady Eleanor Chilton."

Andrew emptied the contents of his glass. "I should

think 'Lady Chill' would be a more apt moniker for the girl.''

The men erupted in laughter.

Mr. Tilney turned the lady's name over in his mind. "Chilton, you say? The girl couldn't be Dessborough's daughter! Now, was there ever a quiz? I know Dessborough. Owns the finest stable in England! Bought one of his chestnuts two years ago and he couldn't have been a more genial man to deal with. How does it happen, then, that his daughter should be such a cool one?''

Lord Trowbridge shook his head and shivered mockingly. "Icy, she is.''

"Arctic," contributed Lord Montfort, swaying gently from the effects of his inebriated state.

Andrew was not precisely sober; his sense of discretion was impaired and he was enjoying a certain fuddled sense of irresponsibility. He had never before been one to bandy a lady's name about a gentlemen's club and had never been one to tolerate such behavior from others. But the memory of Lady Eleanor Chilton's cool blue eyes and frigid demeanor still rankled and effectively outweighed his better judgement. "It occurs to me," he said, "that someone ought to teach the lovely Lady Chill a lesson.''

"Can't be done," said Lord Montfort, pessimistically. "It should take a bonfire to melt such a woman!''

"Ah, don't sell yourself short, Monty!" said Lord Trowbridge. "You're a fiery little man, given the right circumstances!''

Lord Montfort couldn't decide whether to be pleased or angry with his friend's comment. He finally decided that any kind of emotion would require too great an effort for a man in his drunken state. He said in a dramatic tone, "No mortal man could melt the icy heart of Lady Eleanor Chilton!"

"De Ardescote could do it!" said Mr. Tilney with confidence.

Lord Montfort scowled. "I should pay to see it when he does! Can't be done, I tell you, by Andrew or any man!"

Mr. Tilney laughed. "A bit too cocksure, Monty! Andrew has yet to meet the miss whose heart he couldn't melt, I'll wager!"

"Then he hasn't met this one!" said Lord Montfort. "Makes no never mind, I tell you. Andrew, speak up! Say you'll show Monty here how the thing is done!"

"Stuff!" cried Lord Trowbridge, rushing to the defense of his friend, Lord Montfort. "Monty could win her if he had a mind to. He's a prime catch! Chits have been on the scramble for him since he first cut a wheedle!"

Captain Lisle took immediate exception to this speech and said challengingly, "Monty may cut anything he likes, but he doesn't compare to Drew, here. You can't imagine that any girl should prefer to be addressed by Monty over the Fashionable Corinthian!" He glanced up into Lord Montfort's suddenly dark expression and said, hastily, "Well, it's the truth, dash it. You may be a prime catch, Monty, but everyone knows Andrew can double you in fortune and breeding."

"All well and good if wealth were the only thing to be considered," protested Lord Trowbridge. "But women put a great deal of weight on romantic nonsense, and Monty has considerable address in that area!"

"It's true," slurred Lord Montfort with profound sincerity. "I'm a very romantic fellow."

"You're talking through your brandy!" Mr. Tilney accused with a laugh. "Fifty guineas says Andrew will have the lady in his pocket by the end of the Season!"

Lord Montfort drew himself up to his full, but swaying, height. "One hundred guineas says I shall do it in a month!"

Captain Lisle let loose a crow of derision. "Here, now, Andrew! You can't mean to let that challenge slip by!"

Andrew shrugged his great shoulders disinterestedly and returned his attention to shuffling the long-neglected deck of cards. "A trifle. I have found that wagers of less than a thousand pounds are rarely tempting and never to be taken seriously."

Montfort flushed angrily. "Very well, then! Make it a thousand pounds! Trifle, indeed!"

"I don't believe you have considered the matter clearly," said Andrew with a hazy but still intelligent glance at his rival. "After all, how are we to determine when the bet is won? If Monty claims to have the lady in his pocket, I fear I should have to demand proof. Not that I doubt your good word, Monty, but there must be firm evidence of the deed before I should hand over such a sizeable wager."

Lord Montfort almost choked. "Sizeable wager? You've lost treble that amount dropping loose change on the street! I swear, de Ardescote, you are the most complete hand!"

Andrew wagged an admonitory finger. "Nevertheless, I shall demand proof."

"Then name it, sir, and I shall deliver it to you!"

Andrew looked thoughtfully down upon Montfort

from the advantage of his great height and debated for the briefest moment the wisdom of proceeding with such a despicable wager. To engage in such a venture would mean the social ruin of the young lady involved, for her name would be bandied about every club in St. James. He had consumed enough brandy, however, to have rendered him quite drunk. A recklessness seized him, and this, coupled with a strong desire to teach Lady Eleanor Chilton a lesson she would not soon forget, provoked an attraction too strong to be ignored.

He smiled slightly as a sudden notion came to him. "A kiss," he said simply. "To claim victory, the winner must warm Lady Chill with a kiss."

Lord Montfort considered Andrew's proposal with a great effort. "Doesn't seem too difficult."

"Then perhaps I didn't make my meaning clear. You see, I do not speak of a fleeting touch of the lips, stolen when the girl is unsuspectful. No, no! Lady Chill must return the kiss with affection. Only then can we be sure that her icy heart has indeed melted."

"And the thing must be witnessed," exclaimed Captain Lisle, plunging into the thick of it with enthusiasm. He indicated Mr. Tilney, Lord Trowbridge, and himself with a slight gesture. "You must do the deed in front of one of us. Is it agreed?"

Lord Montfort, having crossed the bounds of prudent thought with the last bottle of brandy, did not hesitate to raise his glass in salute. "Agreed."

The other gentlemen raised their glasses as well.

"Then it's sealed," said Andrew and he drained his glass in one gulp. "In thirty days, one of us shall melt the heart of the lovely Lady Chill with a kiss and—cad that I am—I intend it shall be me!"

Chapter Four

Sir Andrew took a fortifying sip of coffee and peered with bleary eyes at his friend across the breakfast table. "Don't plague me now, Lisle! I have a devil of a head."

"I'm not at all surprised," remarked the Captain in a cheerful tone. "I've seen you on the toodle many a time, but never as you were last night. Whatever possessed you to drink such a sum?"

"I don't know," Andrew replied, experiencing great difficulty in conjuring even the vaguest memory of the previous evening. He watched as a footman placed a heaping breakfast plate before Captain Lisle, and said, with obvious revulsion, "Good lord! You don't intend to eat that in *my* presence!"

The Captain smiled back delightedly. "You know, you told me several times last night that you were drunk, but I don't think I quite believed you. Your words weren't the least slurred and you left White's walking straight as an arrow. Poor Montfort had to be carried out!"

"I shouldn't be interested if Montfort *crawled* out of the club," said Andrew, with a faint note of distaste.

"Perhaps not, but I'll wager you're interested in his actions this morning!"

One of Andrew's dark brows rose questioningly. "My dear Lisle, have you ever known me to show the least interest in the comings and goings of a man of Montfort's stamp?"

Captain Lisle looked at him with a good deal of astonishment, and said in a mildly accusing tone, "You don't remember! You don't recall the least bit of what occurred last night, do you?"

"I recall nothing but a good deal of brandy," said Andrew, as he gently massaged his still-throbbing temples.

"But—but what about the wager? Do you recall nothing of that? No, I can see you do not," he said, correctly interpreting Andrew's rather pointed expression. "Then it is fortunate indeed that I am here to remind you, or you might find that Monty has stolen a march on you!"

"Geoffrey, *what* are you talking about?" demanded Andrew with awful patience.

"I'm speaking of the wager you made last night with Montfort. You were in the devil's own pocket over the Chilton girl. You know, the one we met at my Aunt Harpole's ball."

Andrew frowned as a sudden vision of Lady Eleanor Chilton's lovely features swam before his eyes. "Ah, yes!" he murmured. "The Lady Chill!"

"That's the name you called her last night in the

club," said Captain Lisle, convinced that his friend's memory was at last returning.

"Did I indeed? Then I am the veriest bounder! What would have possessed me to bandy a lady's name about White's? Never mind! I know what possessed me. It was the brandy! Go on with your story, Lisle! Of what other despicable behavior am I guilty?"

"Only the wager, but you can't be blamed for that. Montfort did goad you a bit," allowed the Captain, handsomely.

"Much as I am convinced I shall regret it, I suppose I must be told the basis of this wager."

Captain Lisle obligingly described, in explicit detail, the bet Andrew had made with Lord Montfort.

Andrew was very much appalled by what he heard. "Are you telling me that I have made a gently born female the object of a wager?"

"And what a wager it is!" said the Captain, appreciatively. "I have seen you cut out more deserving rivals than Montfort in the pursuit of a lady's affections. Being the first to cross the finish line in this race should be relatively easy for you, I'd say!"

"Don't busy yourself collecting your winnings yet! I have no intention of claiming victory in *this* work!"

"No-No victory?" repeated the Captain, quite astonished. "Here now, Drew, what are you saying?"

"I am saying that Montfort may win the blasted wager," said Andrew firmly. "What kind of blackguard do you take me for, Lisle? Do you think I shall willingly bandy a lady's name about the clubs of St. James? Of course I shall not go through with such a boorish business!"

"Drew, you cannot mean it! Back down from a wager? And with Montfort, of all people?"

"Montfort may claim his winnings and be happy! I shall have no part of it! I assure you, I dismissed the wager as soon as it was made and never gave the matter another thought."

The dining room door opened to admit Mr. Robert Hanshaw, Sir Andrew's secretary. He bowed slightly and said, quite earnestly, "I beg your pardon, Sir Andrew, but I was only just now told you were awake this morning or I would have come to you earlier!"

Andrew regarded his loyal secretary with a frown of confusion. "Come to me sooner?" he repeated. "I have only been downstairs these ten minutes. What possible beastly business have you concocted that should require my attention at this hour of the morning?"

"Well, sir, you did give me very explicit instructions last night that I was to come to you the moment you were up and about this morning," said Mr. Hanshaw gravely. "You said that you knew you might trust me to always do as you asked."

"Did I? And had you any notion at the time I plied you with such praises that I was quite probably foxed?"

"Yes, sir," said Mr. Hanshaw, candidly.

"Then in future I shouldn't recommend that you refine too much upon my instructions whenever you should find me in such a state."

"Yes, but—but I've already carried out your instructions!" said Mr. Hanshaw.

"And I am sure—knowing you as I do—that you have followed those instructions to the letter. Someday you must tell me all about them."

Now it was Mr. Hanshaw's turn to appear confused.

"But—but what about the young lady, sir? The one in Grosvenor Square. Don't you *remember*, sir? Before you retired last night, you ordered two footmen posted outside her house."

Andrew frowned. "Did I? What an extraordinary demand, to be sure! And did I tell you the reason I wanted two of my servants to miss their beds for the opportunity to spend a chilly night on the streets of London?"

"Oh, yes, sir! You were quite candid about it, as a matter of fact. The men were to watch the house in case the Lady Eleanor should come out, and then they were to follow her. And when she reached her destination, one was to stay close by while the other returned to report to you the lady's whereabouts."

Captain Lisle let loose a hoot. "So you forgot all about the wager, did you? Never gave it another thought, eh? For a moment there I quite believed you, you dog! To think I was worried that Montfort might squeeze in on you when all the time you had already conceived a plan of such barefaced piracy!"

Andrew looked quite astounded, prompting Mr. Hanshaw to say, "Lady Eleanor Chilton was followed this morning to Hookham's Library, sir, and is accompanied by another young lady who, from the description you provided last night, I believe to be her cousin."

"Then we are off to Hookham's!" proclaimed the Captain, rising from the table with enthusiasm. "Hanshaw, alert Sir Andrew's valet! You must be out of that dressing gown immediately, Drew!"

"I have no intention of following Lady Eleanor Chilton to a lending library," said Andrew, sternly. "Really,

Lisle, you cannot suppose I would conceive such a plan had I not been deep in my cups!''

"Devil take it, you can't cry off now!'' exclaimed the Captain. "The wager has been recorded in White's Book with Tilney and Trowbridge as witnesses. Why, by evening you shall be nothing but a poor opinion if you lose to Montfort. Only think of the consequences!''

Andrew's thoughts were concerned with that very subject. He was not a man whose pride allowed him to meekly accept defeat in any venture. He had, however, been most willing to do so in this instance because of an overriding sense of chivalry toward the young lady involved. But now he was given to understand that his wager with Montfort, made while under the influence of strong emotion and several bottles of White's best brandy, had been set to the pages of the Betting Book. The thing was now public knowledge, at least within the confines of St. James Street, and he had a sudden notion that the entire population of gentlemen's clubs was awaiting the outcome of the wager.

It was not in his style to admit defeat without so much as a fight, and when his opponent was a man of Lord Montfort's ilk, the notion of surrender chafed, indeed.

He perceived that he was caught in a quandary. If he were to act upon the wager, he would be nothing but a cad. If he were to walk away from the challenge, he could only hope that at best he would be thought to have taken leave of his senses; the worst he could hope was to be labeled a failure. He cared for neither consideration.

A strong sense of injustice swept over him, and he promptly placed the blame for his predicament at the dainty feet of Lady Eleanor Chilton. The memory of her snubs was too fresh, the recollection of her disapproval too strong to be denied. Once again Andrew entertained an overwhelming desire to teach her a lesson.

It would take little effort on his part to prove that she had grossly misjudged him; it would take very little time to convince her that by being uncivil to him, she had allowed to slip through her lovely fingers a golden opportunity to set the fashionable world on its ear.

He had no desire to crush her, for he considered himself too noble for such a paltry revenge; but he didn't think any harm would come of her learning that she had chosen the wrong man to humiliate in front of a crowded *ton* ballroom.

An irrational yet keen desire to see if Lady Eleanor Chilton could be made to regret her actions sustained him during the carriage ride with Captain Lisle to Hookham's Library.

He arrived to find his liveried sentry still posted outside the door of the establishment. Lady Eleanor, it seemed, was still inside.

He found her easily enough. She was engaged in scanning some upper shelves as if she were searching for one particular volume. Her blue eyes were dark with concentration and her smooth, fair brow was furrowed. Her blond hair was caught up in a profusion of curls and her head was tilted back in a manner that left exposed the white column of her slender neck. She presented just as stunning a picture as Andrew remembered from the evening before; but he also recollected, with vivid clarity, the sharpness of her tongue and the coolness of her manner.

He squared his shoulders purposefully and quietly

approached her from behind. When he was at last upon her and was close enough to detect the faint scent of her perfume, he silently reached past her to the upper shelf and grasped a slim book at random. "Do allow me," he said genially. "Is this the volume you seek?"

She turned quickly to face him, her cheeks suddenly flushed and an expression of adorable confusion on her face.

"Sir Andrew! Oh, I—I had no notion you were behind me!" she said in a rush.

She looked up into his eyes and saw an odd expression there that she could not interpret. An unnamed emotion glittered within their brown depths and the memory of her shameful conduct during their first meeting surged back to send another wave of blushing color to her cheeks.

He smiled slightly and his dark brows went up. "Lady Eleanor? Is this the book you were attempting to reach?"

"No! I—I mean, yes! Yes, of course!" she said, determined not to be uncivil a second time by refusing his kind gesture. She took the book from him. "How—how good of you to help me!"

"Your taste in reading matter is quite extraordinary, Lady Eleanor. I had thought your interests might run more toward popular novels."

Eleanor looked down at the title of the book. *The Use of Virginia Creeper in the Body of A Landscape Garden.* "Oh!" she exclaimed, feeling a good deal foolish. "Yes, well, I—that is—thank you so much for handing it down to me!" She stopped and looked up at him again in confusion, for she really had no idea how to proceed. She had been half-convinced that she would never again meet Sir Andrew, for her aunt had made quite clear that the Fashionable Corinthian moved only in the very best circles of Society. Yet there he stood, quite at his ease, looking down upon her with one of the most charming smiles she had ever encountered.

A strong desire to apologize for her previous behavior welled within her, but she could not hit upon the right combination of words. Besides, he didn't appear to be harboring a great resentment toward her or he wouldn't be now regarding her with such calm good grace.

But beneath Andrew's poised expression simmered a good deal of malicious satisfaction. He watched as a steady stream of varying emotions paraded across Eleanor's upturned face. For a brief moment he thought he detected in her lovely expression a doubt, a hesitancy. So, the girl wasn't quite so cocksure as she had made herself out to be! He entertained the fleeting notion that he had been dealt a most favorable hand. If he played it right, his abominable wager with Montfort might be settled a good deal sooner than expected.

Eleanor flashed a tentative smile and struck a fairly safe conversational gambit. "Do you visit the lending library often, Sir Andrew? I don't believe I have had the pleasure of seeing you here before."

He had never before stepped inside the place, but that fact did not deter him from answering, in his most seductive voice, "Not often. But then, it is not in my style to attend come-out balls, either. How do you suppose it should happen, then, that you should be present on the two occasions I am not of my usual habit?"

"Perhaps it is Fate that is intent on thrusting us together," she suggested.

He smiled slightly. She was following his flirtatious

lead so easily. He said in a low, caressing tone, "And for what purpose do you suppose Fate would have us be together?"

She was having a hard time supposing anything, with the handsome Sir Andrew still standing so close to her. His nearness was having a dramatic effect upon her senses and wits.

"I don't know," she managed to say at last. "Perhaps we are meant to be friends."

He was frankly surprised by her answer. He was quite used to watching young ladies fall into a fluttering state of confusion whenever he chose to single them out, and he was also used to hearing himself described by a fair portion of Society's eligible women as nothing short of a matrimonial prize. Lady Eleanor, he realized, was apparently not like most young women, and he was quite thrown off his stride. He didn't speak for a moment, unsure whether to be piqued or diverted by her failure to respond in kind to his flirtatious overtures. A moment's consideration told him it would never do to rush her too quickly toward his jump, and he answered gravely, "Friends, Lady Eleanor? Rest assured, madam, if you are ever in need of a friend here in London, you have but to command me."

She hesitated, debating the believability of his words; then she said, in a rush, "Oh, you have no idea how glad I am to hear you say so! Especially after my horrid behavior last night! Please accept my apologies! I was so abysmally rude and I am deeply ashamed!"

"My dear Lady Eleanor, there is really no need," said Andrew before she could continue. "I had the notion you were not at all happy last night; that you would have preferred to have been anywhere but Lady Harpole's ballroom.''

''Yes, that's it exactly! Only, I was forced to accompany my cousin and my aunt, you see, and—!'' She stopped short, keenly aware that she had spoken impulsively. ''I do beg your pardon!''

''No need,'' said Andrew, affably. ''Have you been much bullied since you came to London?''

''I have been bullied since my father first proposed the trip!'' Eleanor answered, candidly. ''He is the dearest man to me, but he will insist that I have a Season and will brook no argument. I believe he wants me to make a very splendid match with someone eminently suitable! I, on the other hand, want only to go home. My mind is already made up that no one in London shall suit me, you see.''

''Is that so? How very curious. Then you *will* need a friend and I think that friend should be me.''

She eyed him suspiciously for a moment. ''Why?''

''For a number of reasons—all to your advantage, I might add. I shall tell them to you presently, but now I see your cousin approaching. Ah, Miss Glower! How do you do?''

Eleanor turned to find that they had been joined by Iris and Captain Lisle. They exchanged greetings briefly, then Sir Andrew claimed Eleanor's hand and brought the tips of her fingers to his lips.

''Lady Eleanor, I am grateful we have had the chance to further our acquaintance. I hope I may have the pleasure of calling upon you very soon. Perhaps then we may finish our most fascinating conversation.''

Whether it was the promise of seeing him again or the light touch of his lips against her hand that left her feeling breathless, Eleanor could not be quite sure. She was sure, however, that it would never do to reveal the measure of the effect he had upon her, and she immediately adopted what she hoped to be a rather impassive expression.

As soon as Andrew and Captain Lisle had walked out the door, Iris whispered loudly, "Dearest cousin! How did you manage to bring Sir Andrew de Ardescote about? Last night the two of you were at dagger drawing, and today he means to call upon you! If he intends to take you up, perhaps you shall be a success after all!"

"Oh, pooh!" said Eleanor, feeling the need to quell her cousin's transports and to still the odd fluttering of her own heart. "Really, Iris, you refine too much upon the matter! I'm convinced Sir Andrew is merely being polite and has no real intention of calling on me."

Iris frowned. "Why do men think it polite, then, to make promises they have no intention of keeping?"

"I don't know," said Eleanor. "But I for one shall not pine if he *never* sounds the knocker at Glower House."

"But without retrieving Sir Andrew's good opinion, your season is quite ruined," reminded Iris. "Mama said so last night."

"I think I already have retrieved his good opinion. You see, Sir Andrew and I have decided we might be friends." Eleanor's blue eyes lit as an idea, sudden and brilliant, came to her. "If Sir Andrew were my friend, I shouldn't doubt that your mama would be greatly impressed! I daresay she sets great store by his opinion, and if *he* were to recommend that she send me back home, I daresay she would do it!"

Iris regarded her with a baffled expression. "But why would Sir Andrew recommend such a thing, pray?"

"Oh, I am certain he would do it for a *friend*," said Eleanor, confidently. "And I intend to make Sir Andrew my most particular friend, indeed."

Chapter Five

Upon their arrival home, Iris dutifully reported to her mother Eleanor's encounter with Sir Andrew. She was not able to relate the intimate details of their conversation, however, for Captain Lisle, an experienced campaigner, had purposefully intercepted and waylaid Iris with charming though meaningless small talk in order to provide Andrew and Eleanor the chance to speak privately.

Lady Glower was overjoyed at the news. A mere moment before she had resigned herself to the fact that Eleanor's conduct had sent them all irretrievably past bearing in Society's eyes. But now it very much appeared that Sir Andrew, rather than repulsed, was oddly attracted to Eleanor's arctic manners; and where Sir Andrew de Ardescote led, Society was sure to follow. Eleanor thus found herself restored to her aunt's good graces.

By the next morning there was harmony in Glower

House once again, but little rejoicing in Eleanor's heart. She was feeling rather tremulous at the prospect of furthering her friendship with Sir Andrew. The recollection of his nearness as he spoke to her in the library and the way his lips lightly brushed her hand was enough to send her senses curiously fluttering in a way she had not anticipated. An odd sense of guilt compelled her to the small writing table in her sitting room, where she immediately set about penning an impassioned letter to Charles Adair.

Iris entered the room to find her setting the final words to paper. "Dear Cousin, you must come see what has just been delivered downstairs!"

"In a moment," answered Eleanor, her thoughts still on her letter. "I must first send this note off to Charles."

Iris sat down in a nearby chair and sighed deeply. "Is it a protestation of love, Cousin? Do you write to repledge your devotion?"

"Something of that nature," said Eleanor, kindly. "I am writing to ask dear Charles to remain patient, and to tell him that I shall come to him as soon as possible and then we may be married, as we have always planned."

"Do you absolutely *pour* your heart out to him and leave nothing out?" asked Iris, wistfully. "Did you tell him about the balls we have attended and did you write to him of Sir Andrew?"

Eleanor's head came up with a snap. "Write of Sir Andrew? W-Why, no!" she answered, feeling inexplicably guilty. "Why, pray, should I?"

Iris shrugged. "No reason. Perhaps Charles should want to know you have an ally in Sir Andrew. You might tell him of your plan to have Sir Andrew speed your return home.''

"Oh! I—I don't think Charles should be at all interested in that," said Eleanor, battling a twinge of conscience. "I think it would be best if I told him of Sir Andrew's friendship another time."

"Then do, please, come downstairs!" said Iris, jumping to her feet and clasping Eleanor's hand to give it a tug.

Laughing, Eleanor followed her cousin down to the drawing room where Lady Glower was examining a stunning bouquet of flowers that had just been delivered.

"They're for you, dear Cousin!" Iris announced with excitement.

Eleanor could not help but be affected by the beauty of the delicate blooms. "For me? I wonder who could have sent them?"

Lady Glower waved a card aloft. "Lord Montfort sent them. I must say, when I first saw them, I was inclined to think the thing a trifle overdone. A posy would have sufficed! But now I see they are from Montfort, it is perfectly understandable, for he is never one for understatement."

Eleanor frowned as she searched her memory. "Who is Lord Montfort?"

"You were introduced to him at Lady Harpole's ball, my dear," said Lady Glower, helpfully. "A very pleasant-looking young man with side-whiskers and brown hair. I believe you snubbed him dreadfully, so what might have possessed him to send you such a tribute, I really cannot say. How very different things were in my day! When I was a girl, young ladies received such tokens only if they were well behaved!"

Eleanor had only the vaguest memory of Lord Montfort and was at a loss to explain why he might have felt
compelled to send her such a gift. "I wish he had not
done so," she said, rather worriedly, "for he shall expect
me to thank him when next we meet, and to do so
would only encourage him!"

Lady Glower cast her a pointed look. "Lord Montfort
is quite wealthy and comes of a fairly respectable family!
Of course, he can never compare to Sir Andrew. Still,
his suit is not to be scorned."

Eleanor's back went rigid and her chin came up a
bit. "I hope, Aunt, that you do not think I am guilty of
encouraging Sir Andrew, for nothing could be further
from the truth! I assure you that by speaking to me
yesterday at Hookham's, Sir Andrew was merely being
kind. He is a gentleman of the first order!"

She had been thinking, when she uttered those impassioned words, of Sir Andrew's unfailing conduct toward
her during their first meeting at Lady Harpole's ball.
Then he had greeted her every incivility with constant
courtesy, and had spoken pleasantly enough when they
had chanced to meet again at Hookham's Library. But
it wasn't until she perceived the startled look upon the
faces of her aunt and cousin that she turned and realized, with a rush of embarrassment, that the doors to the
drawing room had been thrown open by Lady Glower's
overly efficient butler, and that Sir Andrew de Ardescote
had already entered the room.

If he chanced to have overheard Eleanor's remark,
he chose not to show it, but greeted Lady Glower most
charmingly, then bowed toward Iris and Eleanor.

"How do you do, ma'am? I hope I am not intruding,

but I had a notion to invite Lady Eleanor to drive through the park with me, if that scheme is agreeable."

It was certainly agreeable to Lady Glower, who did not hesitate to accept Sir Andrew's invitation on her niece's behalf. Almost before she knew what was happening, Eleanor was garbed in pelisse, gloves, and bonnet, and was being handed up into Sir Andrew's elegant phaeton. The pressure of his strong hand at her waist brought another tide of color to her cheeks and she took a moment to compose herself while Sir Andrew settled beside her.

They rode in virtual silence until they reached the park. It was still too early in the day for the Fashionable Promenade, so they had the park very much to themselves. Andrew turned onto the carriage path and allowed his pair to pick up their speed a bit.

He glanced down at Eleanor, noting the pale blue bonnet that mirrored the color of her eyes and so fetchingly framed her beautiful face. She seemed to be holding herself in rigid check and he considered that it might be diverting to tease her out of her icy mood.

He said, smoothly, "I am pleased you accepted my invitation this morning. From your expression, though, I cannot help but think you might have preferred to have stayed at home. I wonder, why did you consent to drive out with me?"

She almost jumped, so unexpected were his words and so near was his voice to her ear. She immediately resolved that he should not know how much his closeness disconcerted her and, in a vain attempt to mask her whirling emotions, answered in a too flippant tone, "Oh, I *dare* not decline an invitation from the Fashionable Corinthian! Although I must wonder why you chose to invite *me* to drive out rather than some more worthy damsel.''

Her words missed their mark. Sir Andrew, far from rebuffed, looked down at her and said in a quiet voice of calculated kindness, "It occurred to me that you might be somewhat in disgrace with your aunt after your unfortunate debut at Lady Harpole's ball. It also occurred to me that I might be in the way to smooth some of those hard feelings a bit. That is, after all, something a friend would do, Lady Eleanor. And we have agreed to be friends, have we not?"

She couldn't have felt more wretched if he had slung about her neck a placard that read, *Ingrate.* She looked up at his aristocratic profile and said, "I beg your pardon! I should not be surprised if you decide you will not be my friend after all, when I am guilty of saying the most uncivil things to you!"

He met her look evenly. "Why is that, do you suppose? I have a notion you are trying to warn me off!"

"I am!" she answered confidingly. "Or at least, I *was!* But now that I am sure you have no designs on me—!"

"Designs on you?" he repeated, in a fair imitation of horror. "My dear Lady Eleanor, nothing could be further from the truth!"

She searched his face for a moment, then said, earnestly, "So you do not intend to flirt with me and court me and—and make me an offer of marriage?"

He looked down at her and said, with wholehearted honesty, "No, Lady Eleanor, I do *not* intend to make you an offer!"

"Oh, thank goodness!" she exclaimed, relaxing visibly beside him.

Her obvious relief that she was not to be made the object of his romantic intentions was a turn Andrew had not anticipated. He racked his brain to recall what words he might have said, what deed he might have done, that should have earned him such a low position in her eyes. He could recall nothing and could only suppose that she held him in such aversion because she found him unattractive.

The knowledge that there was a woman in all of England who did not subscribe to the popular notion that Sir Andrew de Ardescote was the perfect man to take as husband was enough to cut him to the core of his self-esteem and leave him furious. All the many feelings that had prompted him to embark upon that abominable bet with Montfort intensified. A mere moment before he had considered the wager nothing but a diversion, a challenge; but now he was resolved to win the bet at any cost. A sudden notion that he could very easily make Eleanor fall in love with him just so his attentions might veer off at the last minute, was a prospect he found too enticing to be denied.

"Tell me, Lady Eleanor," he invited in a silky voice through fairly clenched teeth, "is it *my* attentions you find so repulsive or are you just generally averse to the subject of marriage?"

"Oh, I am already pledged, you see," she answered candidly. Andrew looked at her sharply, a question at the ready, and she said hurriedly, "I am pledged to a dear man I have known all my life. His name is Charles Adair, and I should be his wife by now if only Papa had not forced me to have a Season."

"Ah, that explains your reluctance to come to London,'' said Andrew, piecing together the bits of their conversation at Hookham's Library.

"It also explains my determination to *leave* London," said Eleanor passionately, "but my Aunt Glower will have none of it. She says I must remain in Town and attend all the entertainments as my papa wished. So I have resolved to do just as I am bid, but I shall *not* enjoy myself! And if I should find myself in disgrace because of my horrid behavior, perhaps then my aunt will send me home."

"And how has your scheme fared thus far?"

"For the most part I am most cordially disliked," she said, rather proudly, "with two exceptions."

"I, of course, am the first exception. Who is the other?"

Eleanor's smooth white brow furrowed into a puzzled frown. "His name is Lord Montfort and Aunt assures me we were introduced at Lady Harpole's ball, but I cannot recall his appearance or his face. He sent round a large bouquet of flowers this morning just before you arrived. I'm sure I don't know what I might have done to have won such a tribute for I thought to have conducted myself very poorly, indeed!"

"No gentleman would force such attentions upon a lady who has not shown herself willing to accept them," pronounced Andrew, judging this to be an opportune time to thrust a spoke in Montfort's wheel.

"You are right, of course, for I never gave him the least sign of encouragement. Why then, do you suppose he should send me flowers? I cannot recall what the poor man looks like, but I am convinced I was just as horrid to him as I was to all the others!"

This confession made Andrew smile. "You have raised

an excellent question. Perhaps Lord Montfort's understanding is not at all keen.''

"I believe you must be right for I truly do not want his gifts. But my Aunt Glower was very impressed that Lord Montfort should pay me such attention and she may urge me to accept his suit. What shall I do then? Pray, advise me, Sir Andrew, for I am at a loss to know what course I should take!''

Andrew looked down at her, some witty remark on the tip of his tongue; but when he saw the expression on her face, the remark flew away. To tease her, he realized, would be nothing save a monstrous cruelty. She sat looking up at him, a tremulously brave smile on her lips that was quite at odds with the absurdly anxious look in her eyes. He had the sudden realization that she was very much in earnest; that she had devised her rather pathetic plan to snub the *creme de society* merely so her aunt would have no choice but to send her home, and he was a little sorry for her.

"I believe I may be of help," he said, reassuringly. "You see, I have been about the world somewhat and I think I have a pretty good idea of how you may deter any London dandy with an eye to plaguing you with his suit.''

Eleanor clasped her gloved hands together and looked up at him with shining gratitude. "Only tell me what I am to do! The sooner I may leave London, the sooner I may become Charles's wife.''

"Perhaps you are aware, Lady Eleanor, that I am accounted to be a man of considerable address.''

"Oh, yes! My Aunt Glower told me that everyone in London looks to your lead and you quite set the style for all to follow," said Eleanor, ingenuously. "But I don't see how that may be. You don't seem at all to be the type of man whose likes and opinions should weigh so much that an entire town must be persuaded to follow!''

No sooner had these words escaped her lips then Eleanor was struck by the impropriety of her remark. She looked quickly up at Sir Andrew and saw that his dark eyes were once again glittering, much as they had been when first she had encountered him in Hookham's Library. She saw mockery and a touch of malice in his expression, and she blushed fierily to know she was the cause of it. ''Oh, I beg your pardon! You must truly think me the wretchedest girl alive to have said such a thing!''

A slight pause followed as Andrew, quite unaccustomed to being held in any opinion but the highest, recovered his presence of mind. It wasn't long before he demanded, in a rather thunderous tone, ''Lady Eleanor, do you indeed know who I am? Does my consequence mean *nothing* to you?''

He appeared more baffled than angry, prompting Eleanor to reply in a confiding tone, ''Oh, yes! In fact, I rely upon your consequence to speed my return to Charles.''

The square line of his jaw tightened as he stared straight ahead. ''My dear young woman, it makes very little difference to me whether or not you marry your neighborhood puppy!''

''Yes, but you did say you would be my friend, and I believe it is quite common for friends to help one another, you know,'' replied Eleanor, reasonably. ''I'm sure as a friend I should be very willing to help you out of a ghastly predicament, if only you were to find yourself in such a fix! So I cannot think it a *very* bad thing to ask you to use your influence to help me convince my aunt that I must return to Charles." She chanced a look at him and saw that he was scowling. "Oh, dear! I suppose I should not have said *that* either! I do beg your pardon, Sir Andrew!"

He glanced speculatively down at her. "Now I don't know what to believe! Are you sincerely sorry you spoke in haste? Or do you apologize because you fear that you have set my back up and I might not be quite so willing to help you with your scheme to leave London?"

Now it was Eleanor's turn to be surprised. "What an odious creature you must think me! Although I can hardly blame you after the things I have said to you. I assure you, I am not usually so reckless with my tongue!"

"You shall never convince me of that!" said Andrew, a lighter tone creeping back into his voice. "From the little I know of you, I have reason to believe your tongue is reckless more often than even you may think! But never mind! To be considered reckless is one thing, but if you must insist upon apologizing every other time you open your mouth, I shall begin to think you tiresome. And to be considered tiresome is, I assure you, infinitely worse!"

She would have begged his pardon again, but thought better of it and had to content herself with saying instead, in a meek little voice, "Please, Sir Andrew, will you be good enough to tell me what I am to do?"

After an infuriating moment, laughter welled up within him. He shook his head thoughtfully and said in a baffled tone, "Lady Eleanor, I believe it is very safe for me to say that I have never before met anyone quite like you! From the moment of our first meeting I have been alternately intrigued, nettled, angered, and wholly diverted by your ability to say or do the very thing I should least expect. What an extraordinary young woman you are, to be sure!"

Eleanor looked up at him, unsure whether she should find his words pleasing or insulting. He certainly appeared amused and when he smiled down at her, in a rather confounded sort of way, she was struck by how handsome he was. She couldn't resist smiling back.

"Very well! I shall tell you what you are to do," he said, thoroughly restored to good humor. "Since we have already established the fact that I have no intention of paying my addresses to you, I should think you might perceive that I present no threat to your matrimonial plans. What we must do, then, is ward off all comers while you are forced to remain in town. I am, therefore, at your disposal."

She sincerely doubted that having Sir Andrew de Ard-escote at her beck and call should prove to speed her return to Dessborough Place, but she thought better than to say so. "Thank you," she said in a humble little voice that only underscored her doubtful expression.

As if reading her thoughts, Andrew looked down at her. There was a gleam in his eye and a teasing quality to his voice as he said, "That was very well done! Of course, we both know by now that you hold me in the lowest esteem, but it was very kind of you not to throw it in my face again."

Her back went rigid and she flushed with resentment. "I—I didn't intend—!"

He chuckled softly. "Yes, I know! You didn't intend to insult me and you truly beg my pardon. You know, I have the oddest feeling that by the time I finally hand you up into your carriage to begin your journey back to that florid-faced country squire you are determined to marry, you will have delivered my self-esteem a very thorough pummeling from which I may never recover! But never mind! I am prepared to tell you what you must do. From this moment on, Lady Eleanor, you are to be seen everywhere in my company. In very little time it shall be about town that you are de Ardescote's latest flirt. You will become the fashionable rage, invited to all the best parties, and you shall earn a great deal of attention."

Eleanor looked doubtful. "But if I am to be made very fashionable, Aunt will *never* agree to send me home!"

"My dear Lady Eleanor, are you not aware that if you insist upon waging battle on two fronts, you only deplete your forces that much sooner? You are a victim of the poorest military tactics, for you have been fighting not only your aunt, but society, as well. Only look where it has got you!"

"Oh! Yes, I do see what you mean," said Eleanor, politely, but she still looked worried.

"The lesson to be learned is this: If you must be compelled to stay in London, you might just as well enjoy yourself, knowing that in good time you may at last return home with some happy memories of your stay."

"*Must* I enjoy myself in London?"

He looked at her with genuine surprise. "You mean you truly don't want to? What an extraordinary woman you are!" he said for the second time that day. "Most young ladies would be cast into transports over the mere mention of a London Season!"

"But—but I am pledged to Charles Adair!"

"So you imagine that by enjoying yourself, you are betraying him somehow? I see! Tell me, do you suppose this man—this Adair—is deliberately making himself wretched on *your* account?"

This was a question Eleanor had never before considered. "Well, I—I don't know for a certainty. But I did leave him in the charge of my good friend, Georgianna Turpin, who I trust will keep him from becoming too distressed while I am away."

"Then *you* should not become too distressed, either," said Andrew firmly. "Only do as you please! And if it pleases you to remain arctic and aloof in company, then go right ahead—but *do not* do it with me!"

Eleanor smiled. "I shall be very civil to you from now on," she promised.

"Good God, I hope not! Who will deliver me a crushing setdown when I am in need of one?"

He watched her laugh and look away, and he was struck by how pretty she was and how unconscious she was of her beauty. He said, "At any rate, you might not in future be quite as arctic as you have been, for I think your behavior is rather distressing to Lady Glower. I cannot think it is at all enjoyable to be forever at odds with your aunt!"

"No indeed! She has been so kind to me and I have been a terrible trial to her in return," confided Eleanor, sorrowfully.

"As I suspected! We must restore you to your aunt's good graces. Ah, I see that doubtful look in your eye again! You must have another question for me. Go ahead, ask away!"

"If you are to bring me into fashion, sir, will I not attract more suitors?"

"Perhaps, but they shall veer off if they perceive that my attentions are constant."

"I see," said Eleanor, turning the scheme over in her mind. "I am sure you must be right!"

"From your doubtful expression I can tell you are sure of no such thing," responded Andrew, greatly amused. "But it is good of you to say so, anyway! Well? Shall I take you up, Lady Eleanor, and make you the belle of the Season?"

"Are you quite sure you want to?"

"Yes! Only then shall I be afforded the opportunity to retrieve my character in your eyes!" He laughed again, seeing that she was at a loss for words.

He turned his horses toward the park gates. "Trust me! By the end of the Season, you shall be packing your trunks to return home, having never received the least offer of marriage!"

She smiled, encouraged for the first time since her arrival in London. "I hope you may be right."

"You may depend upon it," he said confidently. "And now, having committed myself to this monstrous folly, I had best return you to your aunt. If you are to dance with me tonight, you shall need your rest this afternoon."

She looked up at him, rather shyly. "You have been very good to me, sir! I hope I shall find a suitable way to express my gratitude."

He returned her look and smiled slightly, but Eleanor thought she detected a hint of that telltale glitter in the dark depths of his eyes.

He said in a confidently seductive tone, "My dear Lady Eleanor! When the time comes, I am sure you shall find a suitable way to thank me, indeed."

Chapter Six

Andrew drove Eleanor back to Grosvenor Square with his conscience greatly eased. The knowledge that Eleanor had already committed her hand to some fellow with whom she had grown up had been most welcome news indeed. With Eleanor safely pledged to another man, Andrew stood in no danger that she might form any romantic notions about him. A mild flirtation, a fleeting kiss, and his business would be done. Sir Andrew de Ardescote would have won his wager, and Lady Eleanor Chilton would be bustled aboard a waiting carriage and dispatched to the country and the open arms of her neighborhood squire. What scheme could be simpler?

He handed her down and solicitously escorted her into the house and up to the drawing room. They entered to find Lady Glower and Iris entertaining a pleasant-looking young man with side-whiskers and brown hair.

Lady Glower, looking quite pink with pleasure, held

out her hand to Andrew, saying, "So you are returned! You must not think, Sir Andrew, that you may keep my dear niece all to yourself! There are others who demand her time and attention. Only see, my dear Eleanor, who has come to call upon you but Lord Montfort!"

So this was Lord Montfort! Eleanor vaguely recalled making his acquaintance at Lady Harpole's ball, but she could not be certain. She was certain, however, that she was rather uncomfortable to find him in her aunt's drawing room so soon after he had sent the bouquet of flowers.

Lord Montfort had risen upon their entrance, ready to greet Lady Eleanor with an extravagant compliment; but at the sight of Sir Andrew at Eleanor's side, those pretty words faded fast away. The baleful look he cast Andrew promised signal vengeance later. For Eleanor, he produced his best smile and came forward to raise her hand to his lips.

"Ah! Lady Eleanor! Pleasure!" he said, bowing over her fingertips.

"How nice to see you again, my lord," she answered, fighting back an impulse to snatch her hand from his grasp, "and how thoughtful you were to have sent me such lovely flowers. We—We have been enjoying them all morning."

Lord Montfort appeared infinitely pleased. "Lovely, ain't they? Reminded me of you, Lady Eleanor. *Had* to send them round!"

He seemed a pleasant enough young man, but still Eleanor could not like him. She had just spent the better part of the day in Andrew's company and could not help but contrast Lord Montfort's dandified appearance and manners with Andrew's charm and impeccable good looks.

Lady Glower smiled beamingly upon her niece. "Lord Montfort was just telling us some wonderful news! My dearest Eleanor, do sit down and join us!"

"Yes, do sit down, Lady Eleanor," said Andrew, solicitously holding a chair for her and earning a fiery glance from Lord Montfort.

Eleanor sat down and Andrew took up a position a little behind her, his hand resting on the back of her chair in a way that left Eleanor keenly aware of his presence. She thought his closeness and the manner in which he stood steadfastly at her side was somehow protective. She stole a quick look at Lord Montfort and thought she detected a certain fury to his expression as he regarded Sir Andrew.

"And what, pray, is the news?" she asked quickly, while wondering if she would end her morning watching two gentlemen engage in a display of fisticuffs in her aunt's drawing room.

"Dearest cousin, there is to be a masked ball!" said Iris, sparkling with excitement. "Do tell her all about it, Lord Montfort!"

The young lord forced a smile above his high starched shirt points. "Just so! Mrs. Beringer is determined to have a masked ball and she's setting the day for the end of the month."

"Oh, and Eleanor! Mama says she might consider allowing us to attend!" said Iris, breathlessly. "Is that not famous?"

Eleanor caught a bit of her cousin's enthusiasm. "I should like very much to attend. Please say we may, Aunt!"

"Now, my dear, I haven't quite made up my mind on the matter," said Lady Glower. "You must know I wouldn't normally consider a masquerade ball to be a suitable entertainment for young girls, but since it is Mrs. Beringer who proposes the idea, I believe I shall have to give the matter my consideration. Sir Andrew, you are a little acquainted with Mrs. Beringer. Shall it be an appropriate affair for my girls?"

"I can understand your hesitation, Lady Glower, but I think you may trust Glory Beringer in this matter. Any masquerade she shall host must be one of considerable fashion. Besides, I believe your daughter and niece are looking forward to attending. It would be a pity to deny them."

"I daresay you are right," said Lady Glower as Eleanor cast Sir Andrew a smile of gratitude. "But we have not yet received an invitation! Mrs. Beringer is not quite of our set, you know, and we may not be invited, after all!"

"Nonsense! You *must* be invited!" said Lord Montfort. "Why, it wouldn't be the same without you there!"

Lady Glower smiled kindly at him. "Very prettily put, my lord. But what do *you* think, Sir Andrew? Is there any chance my dear girls and I may be included in Mrs. Beringer's guest list?"

"I have no doubt she intends to include you, ma'am," said Andrew, gravely.

His opinion evidently carried more weight with Lady Glower than did Lord Montfort's, for at this she smiled and seemed to swell visibly. "I am sure you must be right, Sir Andrew! My girls are, after all, very popular, you know! We have received so many invitations this morning, I cannot *think* to sort through them until I have had an opportunity to rest first! Such social demands can be quite tiresome. But I expect I needn't tell *you*, Sir Andrew!''

Lord Montfort, alarmed by the attention being accorded the wrong visitor, said rather impatiently, "Yes, yes, we're all busy! But then, that's what we expect, ain't it? Wouldn't do to sit home, for then people will think you ain't up to snuff!''

"Yes, I do believe you must be right," said Lady Glower. "I am sure you keep yourself quite busy indeed with one engagement after another, day in and day out! Tell me, Lord Montfort, what interesting plans have you for the rest of the day?''

"Well, now, it just so happens I have made some very delightful plans indeed!" he said, pleased by the sudden turn the conversation had taken. "That's why I'm here, matter of fact. Came to ask Lady Eleanor to drive through the park with me! Fine afternoon! Just the thing to parade in the fresh air!''

Eleanor found herself the sudden center of attention. "Today, Lord Montfort? Oh, that is a delightful scheme, to be sure! I cannot think of a more pleasant way to pass the afternoon." She saw Lord Montfort smile in a very satisfied sort of way, and added hurriedly, "But you see, I have only just returned from driving in the park with Sir Andrew.''

She watched his expression rapidly change to one of comic dismay, and she bit her lip to fight back a smile. It was not, however, in her nature to be cruel, and she added by way of a palliative, "You know, I cannot think I am at all used to Town hours. After last night's ball, I am still quite tired. I think it would be best if I were to rest the remainder of the day if I am to attend another ball tonight. Do forgive me, my lord!''

"Of course!" said Montfort, in a gracious tone that was wholly at odds with the venomous look he aimed at Sir Andrew. "You must be quite done up! A pity!"

"Such is the curse of our weaker sex!" said Lady Glower, mournfully. "We tire too easily!"

Andrew stepped from behind Eleanor's chair. "In that case, we must leave you to your rest. Montfort, may I drop you somewhere?"

Lord Montfort's face colored alarmingly as he realized there was no gracious way to refuse Andrew's invitation. All hopes he held for being alone with Eleanor, without Sir Andrew hovering protectively about her, were quickly dashed. A reckless anger caused his good-byes to be stiff and stilted; and he suffered the odd notion that he had not shown himself to advantage in front of Lady Eleanor. For this, he placed the blame directly at the feet of Sir Andrew.

"Mighty Trojan behavior, I must say!" he said fiercely as he climbed up into the phaeton beside Andrew.

"Why? Because I stole a march on you? Come, come! I envisioned you as a much better sport, Monty!" Andrew waited just long enough for his lordship to settle himself before setting off down the street at a swift pace.

"But driving her out in the middle of the morning, hours before the Fashionable Promenade? What were you thinking?"

"That we would have the park very much to ourselves, which is, of course, exactly what happened. Her attention, then, was focused entirely upon me and not on a parade of passersby."

Lord Montfort appeared very much affected by this line of logic. "A little tête-á-tête, eh? Well, you must know you are going about it all wrong! Women don't care for that sort of thing at all! Hardly the sort of grand romantic gesture that shall end in a kiss, de Ardescote!''

"I am sure you must be right," said Andrew, cordially.

"Now, you take me, for example. I know all about the way women like things done. That's why I sent the flowers round. Made quite an impression, I'd say, and they'll last long after that drive through the park of yours is a mere memory!''

Andrew flicked a disdainful glance at his rival, but said in a controlled voice, "You obviously have the advantage over me, Monty.''

"Well, it was never a fair contest, after all," allowed his lordship. "Oh, I know you've had more than your fill of *chere amies,* and some devilish fine ones, too! But I'd wager there was very little coaxing required to earn a kiss from any of them!''

"One wager at a time, if you please, Monty," said Andrew. "So you judge I am pursuing the fair Lady Eleanor in a manner that cannot possibly win?''

"Exactly! I, on the other hand, am going about it in just the romantic way women like. Sent round those flowers this morning. They'll keep me in her mind for the rest of the day. Very romantic gesture, you know! Next, I intend to send her a poem.''

This disclosure surprised a laugh out of Andrew. "A poem? From *you?*''

"Now, don't go off into a peel, de Ardescote! It's well known that women like that sort of thing! Think of Byron. Every woman sighing and swooning at the mere mention of his name! I tell you, poetry is the way to a woman's heart.''

"And how, dare I ask, is this grand romantic verse of yours progressing?''

"Well, there's the thing! I'm having the devil's own time with it! How do you suppose those flummery fellows come up with such nonsense?"

"I don't know," said Andrew, greatly amused. "But I should hazard a guess that Lady Eleanor will be more affected by your poem than even you may imagine."

Lord Montfort appeared pleased. "I daresay you are right. Of course, being a lady, she won't be able to tell me *exactly* how much she likes it. Modesty and that sort of thing! Here now, de Ardescote, set me down at the corner! I shall walk the rest of the way to White's." He cast Andrew a measuring look. "I suppose I may trust you on your honor as a gentleman not to double-back to Glower House and interrupt Lady Eleanor's rest!"

"On my honor as a gentleman? In that case, you have my solemn oath!" Andrew saw Montfort's face color quickly, but whether it was the result of another spurt of sudden anger or merely from the effort of climbing down from the vehicle, he could not be certain. "As it happens, I am off to pay a call on Mrs. Beringer. There are, you see, three ladies I would like to see included among her guests for the masked ball."

He left Lord Montfort at the curb and turned his horses in the direction of Beringer House. Since Mrs. Beringer had been one of his many flirts in years gone by, he didn't think she would deny his request to send invitations around to Glower House.

It had been too long since last he had seen Glory Beringer. Sophisticated, beautiful and, above all, discreet, she was a woman who knew just how to conduct a flirtation.

How very different was Lady Eleanor Chilton with her wide-eyed impertinence and hurly-burly schemes. She was a young woman who hadn't the least interest in embarking upon a flirtation with him, a fact which still had the power to cause him a good deal of resentment.

He had already decided that it would never do for Eleanor to fall in love with him. Still, he could not quite suppress that hunter's instinct that came to the fore whenever he chanced to dwell upon the fact that she did not seem the least interested in his attentions.

He had the notion that if he were to secure an invitation for her to attend the masquerade, Eleanor might be made to look upon him with a bit more favor. He resolved to use whatever means necessary to ensure Mrs. Beringer included Eleanor's name among her guests. And if, upon receiving that invitation, Eleanor were to smile gratefully at him again in that way she had that made her eyes light up and her soft cheeks glow with pleasure, he should think himself well paid for his efforts.

Chapter Seven

It was later that afternoon when Robert Tilney spied Andrew and Captain Lisle riding near the south gate of Hyde Park. He set a course for them, negotiating his own mount along the crowded riding path, and pulled up abreast of his friends, saying, "You're looking very smug, de Ardescote. I can tell you're up to something. What is it?"

There were few people from whom Sir Andrew de Ardescote would tolerate such impertinence; but for Robert Tilney he cocked a brow and looked down upon him in a quizzing manner. "Smug? You mistake, Robert. A de Ardescote never looks smug."

Mr. Tilney laughed. "No? Then how is it I can almost see the feathers coming out of your mouth? You're plotting something, and I've a good notion it has to do with your pursuit of the Lady Chill!"

"As true as ever twanged," said Captain Lisle. "But

wait until you hear what he's done and you'll allow him to look a bit puff-proud!''

Robert Tilney frowned slightly with an unwelcome thought. "You haven't kissed her yet! Without *me* there to witness?''

"No, no! Not that," said the Captain, "although I shouldn't doubt Drew shall very likely have Lady Chill slung about his neck as soon as she hears the news!''

"What news?" asked Mr. Tilney.

"The masked ball," said Andrew calmly in the face of Captain Lisle's enthusiasm. "It was mentioned to me that the young lady in question dearly wished to attend Glory Beringer's masquerade.''

"Glory Beringer," Mr. Tilney repeated, as an expression of dawning realization crossed his face. "Of course! I seem to recall that she was a friend of yours, de Ardescote.''

"My most *particular* friend, indeed," agreed Andrew, as one dark brow flew meaningfully skyward. "And as an old friend, she was very easily persuaded to add the Glower party to her guest list for the masked ball.''

"Nothing short of genius," approved Mr. Tilney. "Montfort may send his wretched flowers, for all the good they will do him. I daresay by securing that invitation, you may consider yourself several lengths ahead of Montfort in the race to kiss Lady Chill.''

Andrew cast him a measuring glance. "Are you telling me you actually thought our little contest with Montfort would prove to be a close one?''

"Tilney is not yet well enough acquainted with you, Drew," said Captain Lisle. "You must know, Tilney, that Drew never takes a bet he cannot expect to win. Only consider the flies!''

"The flies?" repeated Mr. Tilney, his attention kindled.

"Drew once wagered another man five thousand pounds—a sobering sum, mind you!—over whose bread, dunked in tea, would attract the most flies. Drew won, of course, not having bothered to let his opponent know that he had put five spoons of sugar in his own cup!"

"I have found there is no such thing as luck—except the kind of luck one makes for oneself," said Andrew, indifferently.

Mr. Tilney laughed and looked at Andrew with appreciation. "I should have to be a Bedlamite to back any other but you in a race."

"Don't count your winnings yet. My wager with Montfort is different, for it contains one element over which I have little if any control."

"Ah, the Lady Chill herself," murmured Mr. Tilney. "But surely she cannot prefer Montfort to you!"

"Then you must do me the favor of telling her so. She has already displayed a bruising lack of appreciation for my consequence, and I believe she would well wish me otherwhere for the chance to return home and never be called upon to lay eyes on me again!"

"I shall never understand the workings of the feminine mind!" lamented Captain Lisle, whose study of Lady Eleanor Chilton's odd behavior only served to strengthen his commitment to remain a bachelor the rest of his life. "Can any man ever be a match for a woman's reasoning or—for that matter—her tears?"

Andrew cast him a sidelong glance. "Tears? Geoffrey, what *are* you talking about?"

"I'm speaking of women's tears and how they use

them better than any weapon devised by man! Don't pretend you don't know very well what I mean! We've all had to comfort a weeping female at one point in our lives—it's practically a rite of passage for a man! When I think about it, it's quite uncanny! Women have the ability to produce the most substantial tears with a minimum of effort, and at the time that best suits their needs. You know how it is! Some females get all puffy and red about the nose, which is most unattractive, I assure you! But if the girl is lovely—truly lovely!—she will contrive to cry in the most fetching manner, so the teardrops cling to her lashes and her lips tremble ever so slightly—" He broke off suddenly, perceiving that Andrew was regarding him with an expression of confounded amusement. "You may very well laugh, but I tell you, no man is a match for such tactics!"

"Fortunately, Lady Eleanor does not seem to be cut from the crying cloth," said Andrew, muffling a smile. "From what little knowledge I have of her, I should guess her to be more tenacious than tearful!"

"Oh, yes, she's quite out of the common way," said Mr. Tilney, guiding the conversation back to the topic of foremost importance, "but can she be depended upon to do as she should and kiss you when the time comes? I must tell you, de Ardescote, it's becoming a cursed nuisance to trail after you whenever you have it in your head to see the girl, just on chance she might lose the mastery of herself and throw herself upon you! As it is, Trowbridge and I must follow you about just to ensure we are present if the girl should take such a notion into her head!"

"I can only do my poor best," said Andrew, a hint of asperity in his tone. The discussion had begun to grate upon his temper for some unknown reason. No, he *did* know the reason; and, as always when he chanced to think of it, the reason left his humor far from improved.

Try as he might, Andrew simply could not get beyond the notion that Lady Eleanor Chilton had not readily succumbed to his charms. If history were any sort of indicator, she should by now be quite under his spell and quite pleasantly biddable. She was not, and the realization that he was not faring any better than Lord Montfort in his pursuit of her cast a serious chink in his armor of self-esteem.

He didn't relish having Robert Tilney question his ability to bring the chit around; but the small annoyance he felt over that gentleman's comments flamed into irrational anger at the sight of Lord Montfort himself tooling his phaeton directly toward them along the carriage path.

His lordship had spied Andrew and his companions from some distance off and had immediately set a course for them. The carriage he drove was well sprung and his horses were sweet goers purchased from Tattersalls less than a month before on Andrew's recommendation. He looked the very picture of a Nonpareil—until he set his vehicle in motion. Then he revealed himself as a rather cow-handed whipster, possessing neither the skill nor the refinement of the Corinthian set to which he aspired and to which Andrew belonged.

By the time Lord Montfort had tooled his phaeton alongside Andrew, he had recklessly darted across the path of two other vehicles and had so alarmed one rider's horse that it had begun to caracole dangerously.

Lord Montfort eyed Andrew indignantly, oblivious to the mayhem left in his wake, and exclaimed, "I say, de

Ardescote! I just drove past your cousin, the marquess. The man has never so much as nodded in my direction before and today—just now as I drove past him—he stopped me! Claimed he'll offer me fifty pounds on my word that I shall never drive in the park again! What do you think I should do about it?''

Andrew flicked a look of signal dislike over him. "Hold out until he offers you a hundred," he recommended.

Watching Lord Montfort's face color with impotent anger had somehow lost a great deal of the appeal it once held. Andrew had always thought Montfort an unpleasant fellow and not quite the thing. Certainly he was not a man to be liked and admired, but Andrew had always been able to tolerate Lord Montfort's presence. Montfort was, after all, a man of means, even if his manners were deplorable, and he came from a well-respected family, although his behavior from time to time suggested an appalling lack of breeding.

By comparison, Andrew had always taken a certain amount of pride in his own polished address and unfailing manners. He was, after all, a de Ardescote, and he could no more consider conducting himself in a manner unbecoming a gentleman of his consequence than he would consider embarking upon a journey to the moon. He had until now assumed this distinction to be readily apparent to all. No one, from casual acquaintance to close intimate, would ever make the mistake of lumping Sir Andrew de Ardescote in with the likes of Lord Montfort.

Or so he was used to think. Yet Lady Eleanor Chilton treated him no differently than she treated Montfort or anyone else, that he could tell. She was just as heedless of Andrew's worth as she was unaware of the honor being paid her by his having singled her out. A lowering thought.

Her behavior left him furious, confounded, and . . . *intrigued*. He had never before been made to suffer such treatment, and he found himself wondering what exactly it was going to take to turn Lady Eleanor's pretty little head in his direction. He realized that this was not the first time that very notion had entered his mind. In fact, the woman had developed an uncomfortable habit of intruding on his thoughts and he was damned if he knew why.

Of one thing he was certain, however: he had every intention of proving to Eleanor that she had been mistaken to regard him in the same light as that jackstraw, Montfort.

His lordship was, at that moment, fighting to control his volcanic temper. "I've had all I intend to take from your family for one day, de Ardescote! You've become offensive!"

Andrew peered down upon him with a disdainful look often imitated by aspiring young men of fashion. "So have you. The difference is, I am trying to be, while you can't help it. Drive on, Montfort."

It was beyond his lordship's ability to accept such treatment without firing off at least one rash and desperate round. "You think too much of yourself, de Ardescote! You'll be brought to your knees one day, and— mark me!—I shall be there to see it!"

"Drew! You don't mean to stand such treatment from Montfort!" exclaimed Captain Lisle, watching his lordship drive off in a rather erratic direction.

"What will you have me do, Geoffrey? Drag him from his phaeton and pummel him on the carriage path?"

"Send a message to him in the morning!" suggested the Captain, with deep feeling.

Andrew flicked an impatient look at him. "Pistols with Montfort? Next you'll have me shooting at fish in a barrel!"

"All the more reason to meet him! It's time we were rid of the man! He's been nothing but a blight on the landscape of polite society since he first cut a wheedle!"

"Then, by all means, do it yourself, if you are feeling noble and have a burning desire to benefit mankind," Andrew recommended. "But allow me the pleasure of besting him where I think it shall do the most good—in his pockets."

Mr. Tilney nodded knowingly. "Once again, we return to the subject of the wager! It hangs like a dark and forbidding cloud over your head, de Ardescote!"

Andrew's jaw clenched. "That cloud is about to burst—but Monty shall be the only one to feel the raindrops, for this I pledge: I have no intention of losing!"

Chapter Eight

Lady Glower gave her niece a reproachful look. "Eleanor, do cease craning your neck or you shall be mistaken for a goose! Gracious, child, what are you looking for?"

"Nothing," said Eleanor, abashed and most reluctant to confess that she had been watching the door of the ballroom to see if Sir Andrew de Ardescote had yet arrived. "I was merely trying to determine who among our acquaintance is here tonight."

"You shall see them all presently, I am sure," said Lady Glower, prophetically. "You and Iris are in such fine looks I dare say you shall attract more than your share of attention! Ah, here is Lord Montfort! I am convinced he means to dance with you, my dearest Eleanor!"

He did indeed, and Eleanor, mindful of Andrew's recommendation that she enjoy her London Season while it lasted, allowed Lord Montfort to escort her onto the dance floor to join the next set.

As she moved through the steps of the dance, Eleanor found her attention wandering back toward the doorway. Still, Sir Andrew did not appear, and she realized her enjoyment of the evening was curiously impaired by his absence.

Over the course of the last three days, Andrew had never failed to appear at any of the functions at which Eleanor had been in attendance; then his attention toward her had been so constant as to have drawn speculatively knowing looks from the other guests. Little wonder, she reasoned, that she should feel rather empty without him at her side.

On this night she danced instinctively, paying little if any attention to the music of the dance or to the other couples that surrounded her. Her heart was somewhat troubled and her attention was still on the doorway and the possibility of Andrew's arrival, when a change in the pattern of her steps caused her to turn and face the other side of the ballroom.

There, lounging quite casually against a pillar by the far wall, was Andrew. A sudden swell of happiness surged within her at the sight of him; and so great was her pleasure at seeing him again that it took a moment for her to realize that he appeared far from pleased to see her. His dark eyes followed her every movement; and while his casual pose might have been unconcerned, his expression was alert and he was frowning. How long he had been watching her, she had no idea, but she could think of nothing she might have done that would have made him look at her so. With his critical eye upon her she couldn't possibly enjoy the dance, and she was very grateful when the music finally ended and Lord Montfort escorted her off the dance floor.

She was still reluctantly engaged in conversation with his lordship when she saw Andrew making his way toward her through the crush of gaily chattering guests. He was tall enough to distinguish as he moved through the crowd. His impeccably tailored black coat and pantaloons over a white waistcoat and necktie were an elegant contrast to the extravagant attire of the dandy contingency.

He seemed very unconscious of the attention his presence excited. He paused every so often to exchange a word of greeting with a friend or with one or two acquaintances who grew quite pink with pleasure at the prospect of having fallen under the notice of the Fashionable Corinthian, then he continued his slow, graceful progression toward her.

He reached her side and looked down at her with that glittering look that signaled his displeasure. Rather fearfully, she held out her hand and he took it; but instead of raising it to his lips in greeting, as he so often did in that gallant way of his, he tucked it into the crook of his arm. Without so much as a word to either Eleanor or Lord Montfort, he led her out onto the dance floor.

Andrew circled her small waist with one arm and took her right hand in his as the first chords of a waltz sounded. He was a graceful dancer and Eleanor moved effortlessly in his arms, but she was rather piqued that he had not yet spoken one civil word to her and had yet again taken for granted that she would want to dance with him without so much as a proper invitation. She resolved that he may glitter as much as he liked, but she would not suffer because of it. Mulishly, her chin came up a bit, but even then she was so much shorter than he that she was afforded only a clear view of his white neckcloth.

For the first time since Andrew entered the ballroom, the glittering quality left his dark eyes. He wondered if he would ever fail to be intrigued by that delicately militant set to her chin or if he would ever cease to regard her as a refreshing change from the usual pack of blushing, simpering come-out chits. Combative little kitten! She had, quite unintentionally, restored his good humor merely by lifting her chin to that martial angle. The feeling of resentment that had so unexpectedly flared when first he had seen her dancing with Montfort paled to little more than a memory as he tightened his hold of her small waist and swept her into the next turn.

"I see you are admiring my neckcloth, Lady Eleanor," he said at last. "It is a new arrangement, and I think it shall be all the crack in a very short time. I call it, The Arctic Lady."

Eleanor looked quickly up at him. His voice had been grave but his eyes were alight with amusement, as if he alone were privy to some colossal joke. It was nearly impossible for her to maintain a frigid pose when he looked down at her in just that way, but she vowed that he wouldn't know it.

"I may admire your neckcloth, but I do not admire your manners," she said in a voice that sounded more petulant than she would have liked. The censure she had read in his eyes earlier had been oddly hurtful, and she was at a loss to know what she might have done to have earned his displeasure. She was determined, however, that his cavalier behavior should not go unpunished and she said, pointedly, "At least Lord

Montfort *asked* me to dance before leading me onto the dance floor!''

Andrew was far from crushed by this observation. ''Did he, indeed? Excellent! If Monty continues to improve, he may be allowed out in society more often! Tell me, did he dance well?''

Eleanor suffered the odd notion that he was teasing her, that he was keenly aware of the fact that Eleanor had found it necessary to twice remind Lord Montfort of his steps in the dance. She looked up into Andrew's dark eyes and said, with flawed sincerity, ''His lordship was a most excellent partner!''

''I'm glad,'' said Andrew, not bothering to hide his amusement.

It was the first time Eleanor had ever seen him so entertained and relaxed. She had always thought him handsome and now, with his expression cleared and one dark brow cocked at an intriguing angle, she realized that he really did have a charming smile.

He also had a firm hold of her waist, and when his long fingers moved slightly against her back, a curious sensation fluttered deep within her.

She dipped her head to hide a telltale blush and Andrew contented himself for the moment with admiring the intricate arrangement of the golden curls on top of her head. Before long he found the lure of looking into her clear, blue eyes too strong to be ignored and asked, ''How many young jackanapes have been paying you compliments tonight, I wonder?''

Her head came up quickly. ''Why, none! Except, of course, for Lord Montfort. I'm afraid, however, that his compliments were more foolish than flattering.''

''I am not surprised. Men often dissolve into foolishness when attempting to compliment a lovely young woman on the exquisite picture she presents.''

Eleanor looked up at him in astonishment. Gone was all trace of the smile that had tugged at the corners of his lips but moments before. Gone, too, was the teasing tone to his voice, for he had spoken quietly and with perfect sincerity.

For a moment she was baffled, unsure whether he was flirting with her or merely trying to put her at her ease, as any friend might do. She bit back an impulse to ask him if he did indeed think her an exquisite picture; and turned her head quickly away lest he should see how much confusion his simple words had caused her.

They finished their dance in silence. Andrew escorted her to where Iris and Captain Lisle were standing together in conversation, having themselves just left the dance floor. As soon as the chords of the next dance were struck, Captain Lisle very prettily invited Eleanor to join him in the next set.

Andrew watched her walk away on the arm of his best friend and found himself wishing, for the briefest moment, that she had found some excuse to remain by his side. Instead, Miss Iris Glower was standing with him and his impeccable manners dictated that he ask her to be his partner in the next dance. He bowed low and offered his arm and Iris, blushing a fiery color, joined him on the dance floor.

Andrew regretted almost immediately that innate sense of courtesy that had prompted him to dance with Iris. His thoughts were still on Eleanor and the way she had first scolded him, then tried to hide her blushes when he had flirted with her.

Iris blushed, as well, but for a different reason. She was shy in his presence, refusing to so much as meet his eye; and she was rather tongue-tied whenever the steps of the dance allowed for conversation. Andrew's attempts to put her at her ease went largely unrewarded. It wasn't until he had the good luck to ask Iris how she enjoyed having her Cousin Eleanor to stay with her in London that Iris suddenly became quite animated.

"Oh, my dear cousin is a wonderful companion to me and is so enjoying her visit to London! I don't believe, however, that she shall be truly happy until she is at last able to return home. I daresay you know all about that, for she mentioned that you intend to help her in that regard," said Iris.

One of Andrew's dark brows flew questioningly. "Did she, indeed?"

"Oh, yes! How kind you are to come to her assistance! I feel sure that with your help, she shall have her heart's desire and in a very short time everything shall come about exactly as it should!"

"Indeed," said Andrew in a bland voice that would have signaled to a more clever person that this conversational vein would be best left unexplored.

"I suspect you know that my cousin *pines* for the day she shall be with Charles Adair," said Iris, breathlessly. "Has she mentioned that she means to marry him as soon as she returns to her home? She's quite devoted to him, you know, and has been for some time. I believe," she added, feeling a certain amount of embellishment necessary, "that she harbors quite a *passionate* love for him!"

A distinctly sardonic look glittered in the depths of Andrew's eyes, but he said with perfect address, "Now that I think of it, she did mention something of the like.''

"I believe her thoughts are never far from him. How tragic that she cannot be with him now with only his letters to assuage her breaking heart. And, of course, she writes to him almost every day!" Iris said, taking comfort in the fact that she had exaggerated the truth only a little.

The movement of the dance forced them apart, a fact which Andrew considered a timely blessing. Iris's breathless, romanticized disclosures had provoked within him a surprisingly deep resentment. It had never before occurred to him that Eleanor might be in love with that neighborhood puppy she planned to marry. He had considered that match nothing more than an arrangement, a convenience; but the sudden notion that Eleanor might be romantically committed was enough to send a bruising sense of injury through him.

He felt very much as he had upon entering the ballroom earlier that evening to find Eleanor moving gracefully across the dance floor on the arm of Lord Montfort. Some unexplained emotion curiously akin to anger had flared within him then, and took possession of him once again at the mention of Charles Adair's name.

It wasn't like him to engage in such irrational behavior. To be heartened by news of a lady's betrothal, as he had been that morning while driving her in the park, only to be resentful of that lady's marriage plans later in the very same week was not the sort of behavior in which he normally found himself engaged.

The resentment he felt lingered through the remainder of the dance. He had no notion, however, that his dark mood was reflected in his expression until his reverie was interrupted by Lord Montfort at his elbow, saying, "You look like the very devil, de Ardescote! Everyone knows this sort of entertainment ain't in your line, but as long as you're here, you might try to put a pretty face on it!"

These words served to seal his anger. Andrew flicked a look of patent dislike at the young lord, but decided that his remark was not worthy of a reply.

Lord Montfort colored a bit under the weight of Andrew's stare. "Well, don't poker up at me, de Ardescote! After all, I'm in the same curst position as you! It's that girl, I tell you! Can't seem to make the least headway with her, no matter what tactic I try. She don't care for flattery and she don't like gifts. I tell you, the chit's not normal!"

"I believe you may be right," said Andrew, quietly, his attention firmly fixed upon Eleanor as she moved across the dance floor with yet another attentive partner. "She is certainly out of the common way."

"So you agree with me! Then you ain't any closer to winning the wager than I am!" said Montfort, almost crowing. "I daresay, however, that tomorrow shall see a change in our little competition."

Andrew's eyes glittered down upon him from the advantage of his great height. "What happens tomorrow?"

"I shall read Lady Eleanor my poem. It's almost finished and I mean to take it round first thing."

Andrew couldn't help but smile slightly. "I wish you well with it, Monty. Forgive me if I tell you that I don't believe the lady is of a sufficiently romantic turn of mind to appreciate all the poem represents."

"Oh, she'll be romantic enough once she hears my

poem!'' said Montfort prophetically. ''I shall be on one knee as I read it to her. Why, the girl would have to possess a heart of stone not to be affected by *that* sort of gesture!''

''I've no doubt she shall be deeply affected by the scene you just described,'' said Andrew, ambiguously.

Lord Montfort smiled brightly. ''Well, then! Prepare yourself to see me as the front-runner in our little race. I've a strong suspicion I shall win a kiss from Lady Eleanor before tomorrow's day is done!''

Chapter Nine

Eleanor tried to free her hand from Lord Montfort's grasp by giving it a slight and sudden tug. His hold remained firm.

"Please, my lord! You—you must let me go!"

"Dash it, Eleanor, can't you see I am in earnest? After all, it isn't every day that a man pens the sort of nonsense I just read to you!"

Eleanor gave her hand another tug and wished for the hundredth time that her aunt had been a bit more diligent in her duties as a chaperone and had remained in the room during his lordship's visit. "Oh, your poem was . . . ! Words can't express—! Forgive me, my lord, but I am too touched by your gesture to be properly grateful," she said, thinking it wise to appease the young lord if it meant his departure might be hastened.

Lord Montfort frowned. "Well, I must say, I hadn't thought the thing would throw you into a stupor! It's just a poem, after all, and I did write it myself!"

"And I appreciate your efforts very much," Eleanor assured him quickly. "I don't believe I have ever before been the object of such a . . . a grand gesture!"

Lord Montfort was genuinely disappointed. He had read his poem to Eleanor as planned. Although he had never been naive enough to suppose that she would react by throwing herself against him and showering him with kisses, spurred by sudden love, neither had he supposed that she would offer up no reaction at all.

Eleanor had, in fact, been too stunned to make any response when Lord Montfort had first read his ridiculous poem. It took her some moments to realize that it was meant to serve as a protestation of his affections for her, but by that time her efforts were too consumed with holding back a desire to laugh for her to say anything in response.

"Here now! I know what's wrong," said Montfort, with sudden realization as he dipped down on one knee before her. His right hand tightened about her fingers, while in his left he held aloft the paper on which he had penned the verse. "By Jove, I forgot to kneel when I read my poem to you! Never fear! I shall read it again. Prepare yourself to know the full impact of the thing!"

"My lord, I beg you will not!" cried Eleanor, snatching the paper from his hand and vainly trying to keep the laughter from her voice. "Please! Please get up! I shall keep the poem and treasure it always as a memory of this moment!"

"Well, I must say, that's a bit more like it!" said Lord Montfort, getting to his feet. He pressed Eleanor's hand to his lips, then looked into her eyes, bright with unshed tears of laughter. "I daresay I've melted your heart more than a bit with this morning's work. Yes, you keep that poem and whenever you read it, think of me!''

"Oh, I certainly shall,'' promised Eleanor, with little difficulty.

"You've made me the happiest of men. Dare I hope I shall have the pleasure of seeing you this evening at Almack's Gala Night?"

"Yes, I shall be there. And, yes, I shall promise you a dance, if only you will not write any more poetry!''

Lord Montfort's face colored suddenly. "You—you didn't like it!" he accused.

"Oh, no, my lord,'' said Eleanor quickly. "It is only that this is my first time to receive a poem written in my honor. Any other such tributes can only pale in comparison!''

A rather self-satisfied smile touched his lordship's lips. "Until tonight, then,'' he said, finally relinquishing his hold of her hand.

When Eleanor was at last alone she read the poem again. It really was a horrid bit of nonsense, the mere thought of which should prove to be a source of amusement for some time to come. She had a sudden and horrifying thought that perhaps the poem served as a signal that Lord Montfort intended to court her in earnest. She certainly hoped that was not the case and realized, after a bit more reflection, that she had missed a golden opportunity to thwart his suit.

She was, after all, already betrothed to Charles Adair. Surely Lord Montfort would realize that he must not make up to a woman who had already pledged her hand and heart to another! She resolved to tell Lord Montfort that very evening about her plan to marry Charles if he showed the least sign of pursuing her.

Eleanor was given an opportunity to exercise that resolve immediately upon her arrival at Almack's. No sooner had she stepped across the threshold of that most fashionable assembly than her clear, blue eyes scanned the crowd, looking for Andrew. He was not in attendance, but Lord Montfort was and he stepped before her, eager and determined to engage her for a dance.

"I should like very much to dance with you," said Eleanor politely, "but first could we not find a quiet spot where we might talk for a little while, just the two of us?"

Lord Montfort's face lit with what he perceived to be a sudden stroke of fortune. "I should say we might! Here, let me take you away from the crush, Lady Eleanor," he said, offering his arm and leading her into another room where some rather uncomfortable rout chairs were set up near a table of refreshments.

Eleanor sat down and debated for a moment on how best to proceed. She said at last, "I want to speak to you about the poem, my lord."

Lord Montfort captured her hand and smiled triumphantly. "By Jove, I knew that bit of paper would bring you around! Nothing like some lines of romantic nonsense to sway a lady, I always say!"

"But that is what I wish to tell you, my lord," said Eleanor quickly. "You see, my heart has *not* been swayed, at least, not in the manner you would wish. I fear I have given you false hope, my lord."

He frowned suddenly and looked at her askance. "Here, now, what trickery is this?"

"It's not a trick, my lord! I only wish to tell you that I am already committed to another." She saw that his face had gone dark with outraged emotion and she said, softly, "As fine a gentleman as you are, my lord, I fear I could never return your affections."

"So that's the lay of it, eh?" said Montfort, dropping her hand as if it were on fire. "You've set your cap in de Ardescote's direction!"

Eleanor's blue eyes widened in surprise. "Why, not at all, my lord!"

"Enough protesting, if you please! I've seen the way you look at him enough times to know! Don't think, however, that you're the first to set a parson's trap for that man, nor shall you be the last! He don't like green girls fresh from the country. You'll get no offer of marriage from de Ardescote, I assure you!"

"My lord, you quite mistake me," said Eleanor, weak with the shock of his sudden tirade. "I am pledged to marry Mr. Charles Adair, a gentleman I have known all my life and with whom I grew up."

The fury was gone from Lord Montfort's face as quickly as it had come. "Oh? Marry another? Not scrambling after de Ardescote? Well, now, that *does* change things a bit, don't it? Yes, I should say so, indeed."

"I—I do hope you are not disappointed, my lord," said Eleanor, rather tentatively.

"I shouldn't think so," said his lordship. "After all, as long as you're not dangling after de Ardescote, I still have a sporting chance. I say, Eleanor, shall we have that dance now?"

Too baffled by Lord Montfort's mercurial emotions and cryptic words, Eleanor could do little more than place her hand in his and join him on the dance floor.

She moved through the steps of the dance as if in a daze, all the while turning over in her mind his lordship's words. Yes, she thought Andrew handsome; and yes, she thought him gracious and charming; but it wasn't until Lord Montfort's outburst that she realized how often Andrew intruded on her thoughts. His was the last image that swam before her eyes when she fell asleep at night, and the first recognizable image to come to mind when she awoke in the morning. Whenever she entered any assembly, his was the first face she sought in the crowd; and his appearance at her side made even the dullest entertainment a happy event. Even now she missed him, and that realization came to her as a distinct shock.

Lord Montfort returned Eleanor to her aunt's side as soon as their dance ended. Thereafter she refused all other offers to dance, preferring to remain against the wall dwelling irrationally on Lord Montfort's assurance that Andrew had no intention of making her an offer. She never for a moment doubted his lordship's words for he was, after all, Andrew's friend by all accounts. Certainly, they always appeared together whenever she saw them, and she reasoned that Andrew must have confided his feelings to Lord Montfort. A curious feeling of dejection settled over her.

Iris paused long enough between dances to try to cheer her, without success. Lady Glower ignored Eleanor's sudden melancholy, judging her niece's withdrawal to be nothing more than a relapse into her habitual arctic pose.

Eleanor's thoughts were still on Andrew when she heard his distinctly deep voice beside her, saying, "How is it I find the evening's most desirable partner sitting out dance after dance?"

Startled, she rose quickly and looked up to see the

slightest of smiles tugging at his lips. Powerless to resist, she smiled back. "Sir Andrew! I—I had no idea you were here tonight!"

"I've only just arrived. Happy to see me? You must be, or else you'd be dancing until your delicate little feet were gone sore."

That speech, it seemed, was intended as a form of invitation, but he didn't wait for a reply. He tucked Eleanor's hand firmly in the crook of his arm and led her out onto the dance floor as the fiddlers struck the first chords of a waltz.

As he had many times before, Andrew clasped his strong arm about her waist and set her feet in motion. They had taken a full turn about the room before he spoke again.

"Do you know, I had not planned to attend tonight, knowing you would be here?"

"And why, pray, is that?" asked Eleanor, unsure if she should be diverted or vexed by his confession.

"I had a notion it might not do for us to be seen too much in each other's company."

"But I thought it was our plan that we should be in constant company, so everyone shall believe me to be your latest flirt," said Eleanor, reasonably.

He examined her upturned face with surprising gravity. "Shall you mind if people speak of you so?"

"I don't believe so," she answered, having considered the question quite thoroughly. "After all, in a very short time I shall be back at Dessborough Place and married to Charles. I shall not care then what people may say of me now!"

"Very well said," commended Andrew. "I hope you

shall retain a bit of your pluck when you are married at last to your country squire."

Eleanor caught her breath as he swept her into the next turn. "I daresay we shall deal extremely well together," she said after a dizzyingly delightful moment. "Charles doesn't care a fig if I should gain a reputation in London for being a flirt, as long as I return to him as planned. I assure you, you need have no scruples where I am concerned."

"Good, for I haven't any," said Andrew with a flinty look to his eye. "You might as well know, I am something of a bounder when it comes to females."

Eleanor looked up at him sharply. She had the unnerving thought that he was attempting to steer the conversation down a particular avenue for a specific purpose. "Are you indeed? I do not think that may be so, for you have always been the very pink of gentleman-liness with me. Lord Montfort, on the other hand, has made himself something of a nuisance."

Andrew's attention kindled. "Has he been playing the moth to your flame? Shall I swat him for you?"

Eleanor laughed happily. "There is no need, as it happens. I believe I have convinced him that I can never return his affections."

"His affections?" echoed Andrew with a slight frown. "Has he declared himself?"

"Not exactly. But he has made me the very clear object of his attentions. You see, he has written me a poem."

Once again that hint of a smile tugged at Andrew's lips. "I daresay I have a very good idea of the thing, never having read it. No doubt the wretched business is titled, 'Ode to A Mole on A Lady's Brow.'"

"Sir! I haven't any mole!" exclaimed Eleanor, trying to sound severe and failing miserably.

"No. No, you haven't," he murmured, as his dark eyes examined every inch of her clear and happily flushed countenance, as if committing her to memory.

He tightened his hold of her as they entered the next turn and Eleanor gave herself up to the joy and exhilaration of being in his arms.

Andrew watched her appreciatively. Certainly, she was the same young lady who had looked down her nose at him in that icy manner when first they met; but all traces of her stoic reserve were gone now. He didn't think he had ever held a lovelier or happier young woman in his arms; and he knew instinctively that he was the cause of much of her happiness.

He hadn't planned to attend Almack's Assembly, knowing she would be there. He wanted to see if she would miss him if he were not on hand to squire her about the dance floor. In the end, no amount of restraint or resolve could keep him away, and he had found himself climbing the dark stairway to the assembly rooms before he even realized what he was about.

As it happened, fortune had been on his side, for he had had his answer. She *had* missed him. He had seen it on her face the moment her eyes had met his; for he considered it a fairly safe venture to believe that Eleanor would not have glowed quite so much upon seeing him if she were indeed in love with that country squire of hers.

So she was not indifferent to him! That knowledge left him with a great deal of satisfaction. Before long he would be able to claim her soft, pink lips in a kiss and then collect his winnings from Montfort.

With any luck, the dastardly business would be completed in a week. With any luck, he would be a thousand pounds richer and Eleanor would be none the wiser. With any luck, he would be able to suppress for a little while longer that uneasy feeling niggling away at his conscience.

Chapter Ten

Lady Glower happily waved aloft yet another stack of invitations. "Just look, my dears, what has arrived only this morning! I tell you, I never dreamed of such success!" She smiled affectionately upon her daughter and said, "I predict we shall see you betrothed by the end of the season, my dearest child. And you, Eleanor—is it any wonder your papa calls you his minx? How sly you are! To think I was quite overset by your frigid manner, when all the while you were plotting to bring the great Sir Andrew de Ardescote to heel!"

Eleanor looked quickly up from the letter she had been working on at the small lady's writing table and said in a horrified voice, "Oh, no, Aunt! That was not my intention at all!"

Lady Glower would hear none of it. "My dear, you must not be such a modest girl! I congratulate you on your stunning conquest! Now do busy yourselves this morning, children, while I pen our replies to these cards. You know, I have a feeling there is among these an invitation to Glory Beringer's masked ball! And for that we have only Eleanor to thank for so prettily begging Sir Andrew to intervene on our behalf."

"That is not so!" exclaimed Eleanor hotly, but Lady Glower had already left the room. Eleanor turned wide, horrified eyes upon her cousin. "Iris, tell your mother that is simply not so! Beg Sir Andrew, indeed! As if I would ever do such a thing!"

Iris was far from sympathetic. "What does it matter how we obtain the invitation, as long as we may go? I tell you, I have *dreamed* of attending the masked ball. It shall be so—so *romantic!*"

Eleanor scowled. "I hardly think it romantic to have *begged* an invitation."

"Now what, pray, has put you in such a pelter? I've never seen you so cross without reason. Yes, I know," added Iris hurriedly after a rather pointed look from Eleanor, "you did not ask Sir Andrew to obtain an invitation for us. Still, you must admit that he asked Mrs. Beringer to invite us only because he knew it should please you."

"That is not true," said Eleanor, feeling oddly defensive. "I am convinced he asked Mrs. Beringer to invite us because he knew it would bring pleasure to us all. He is kind to a great many people, I believe."

"Then you believe incorrectly," said Iris, "for I have heard that Sir Andrew has never before been known for his benevolence. From all accounts, he is more apt to snub innocent young ladies than to take them up and bring them into fashion."

Eleanor, too, had heard the rumors regarding Sir Andrew's reputation with young ladies, but thought bet-

We'd Like to Invite You to Subscribe to Zebra's Regency Romance Book Club and Give You a Gift of 4 Free Books as Your Introduction! *(Worth $18.49!)*

If you're a Regency lover, imagine the joy of getting 4 FREE Zebra Regency Romances and then the chance to have these lovely stories delivered to your home each month at the lowest prices available! Well, that's our offer to you and here's how you benefit by becoming a Zebra Home Subscription Service subscriber:

- 4 FREE Introductory Regency Romances are delivered to your doorstep
- 4 BRAND NEW Regencies are then delivered each month (usually before they're available in bookstores)
- Subscribers save almost $4.00 every month
- Home delivery is always FREE
- You also receive a FREE monthly newsletter, *Zebra/Pinnacle Romance News* which features author profiles, contests, subscriber benefits, book previews and more
- No risks or obligations...in other words you can cancel whenever you wish with no questions asked

Join the thousands of readers who enjoy the savings and convenience offered to Regency Romance subscribers. After your initial introductory shipment, you receive 4 brand-new Zebra Regency Romances each month to examine for 10 days. Then, if you decide to keep the books, you'll pay the preferred subscriber's price of just $3.65 per title. That's only $14.60 for all 4 books and there's never an extra charge for shipping and handling.

It's a no-lose proposition, so return the FREE BOOK CERTIFICATE today!

Say Yes to 4 Free Books!

COMPLETE AND RETURN THE ORDER CARD TO RECEIVE THIS $18.49 VALUE, ABSOLUTELY FREE!

(If the certificate is missing below, write to:
Zebra Home Subscription Service, Inc.,
120 Brighton Road, P.O. Box 5214, Clifton, New Jersey 07015-5214)

FREE BOOK CERTIFICATE

YES! Please rush me 4 Zebra Regency Romances without cost or obligation. I understand that each month thereafter I will be able to preview 4 brand-new Regency Romances FREE for 10 days. Then, if I should decide to keep them, I will pay the money-saving preferred subscriber's price of just $14.60 for all 4...that's a savings of almost $4 off the publisher's price with no additional charge for shipping and handling. I may return any shipment within 10 days and owe nothing, and I may cancel this subscription at any time. My 4 FREE books will be mine to keep in any case.

Name _____

Address _____ Apt. _____

City _____ State _____ Zip _____

Telephone ( ) _____

Signature _____
(If under 18, parent or guardian must sign.)

RF0396

Terms and prices subject to change. Orders subject to acceptance by Zebra Home Subscription Service, Inc.

AFFIX STAMP HERE

ZEBRA HOME SUBSCRIPTION SERVICE, INC.

120 BRIGHTON ROAD

P.O. BOX 5214

CLIFTON, NEW JERSEY 07015-5214

ter than to say so. She said instead, in what she hoped to be a tone of unconcern, "Sir Andrew may do as he likes. I'm sure I never give him a second thought."

"That's odd. There are some who believe Sir Andrew is quite smitten with you."

Eleanor felt a dull flush of heat across her cheeks. "Iris Glower, I shall thank you not to repeat such horrid gossip!"

"Well, you needn't snap my nose off! After all, I am only telling you what I have heard from others!" said Iris, defensively.

Eleanor was immediately sorry. "I beg your pardon for I didn't mean to be so cross with you. It is just that I have never before been the subject of such speculation and it is rather oversetting."

Iris gave her a searching look. "*Is* it just gossip? Forgive me, cousin, but you must admit that you have seen Sir Andrew every day for the past two weeks. He calls to take you to parties or for rides in the park. At every ball or assembly he stands up with you at least once and very often twice. And, if I am not mistaken, you appear to be quite happy to see him every time!"

Eleanor made a great show of picking up her pen and setting to work once again on the letter she had been writing, as she said with a great deal of reserve, "Sir Andrew is a friend and I should be no more happy to see him than I would any other friend."

"Oh," said Iris, greatly disappointed. "Then you still intend to return to Dessborough Place and marry Charles Adair?"

"Of course," replied Eleanor with firm resolve. "My plans have not altered in the least merely because Sir

Andrew de Ardescote considers me a desirable dance partner.''

Iris took a seat beside her cousin at the small writing table and rested her chin in her hand in a dreamy fashion. "Do you still write Charles almost every day?"

"As a matter of fact, I am writing him now. And he writes me back whenever he is able."

"And does he pour out his heart and write of his longing for you?" asked Iris, hopefully.

"Charles has far too many pressing matters to deal with to find time for such mummery," skirted Eleanor.

"How lucky you are!" said Iris, with a deep sigh. "Some day I hope to have a young man write to me of his undying devotion and I hope he may write volumes and volumes."

Eleanor smiled slightly. "And I hope you may have your wish. You're such a hopeless romantic, dear cousin!"

"I know, but I cannot help myself," said Iris, resigned to her fate. Her eyes caught sight of a small sheaf of pages on the desk. "Is this the last letter you had from Charles? Oh, please! May I read it?"

"Yes, do! If only you will let me finish this letter I have been working on all morning!" Eleanor immediately regretted the impatience with which she had spoken to Iris, but her cousin didn't seem to notice. Instead, Iris happily claimed Charles Adair's letter and began reading as if it held all the entertainment of one of her treasured novels from the lending library.

Eleanor returned to her work and tried to finish her letter. She was having a difficult time of it, for she had realized, as soon she began putting pen to paper, that the now-familiar task of pledging her devotion in a heartfelt letter had somehow lost a good deal of its appeal.

Several times she had toyed with the notion of writing to Charles of her friendship with Sir Andrew, but she could never quite bring herself to do so. How, indeed, did a young lady tell the gentleman she had promised to marry how much enjoyment she derived from the company of another man?

She tried to conjure a mental picture of Charles, patiently waiting at home for her return. Instead, a vision of Andrew, his dark brow at half-cock and the hint of a smile playing at the corner of his lips, swam before her eyes. An undeniable feeling of guilt threatened to settle upon her. She fought it as best she could, by setting her pen in motion with a good deal more determination and speed.

"Eleanor, who is Georgianna Turpin?" asked Iris suddenly, her brows knit into a frown of confusion and the letter she was reading held poised in midair.

"Georgianna is a friend from a neighboring estate," answered Eleanor, her attention still focused on her work.

"But why does Charles write of *her*?" pursued Iris.

"Because both Charles and I count Georgianna as a friend," said Eleanor with great patience. "The three of us have been neighbors for many years and when I left to come to London, I charged Georgianna with doing her very best to ensure that Charles would not miss me too much while I was away."

"Oh," said Iris, accepting the logic of this explanation; but when she turned her attention back to the letter and reread a portion of it, her frown returned. "Eleanor, he mentions her quite often in his letter.

Don't you think it curious that Charles should mention another woman in his letter to *you?*"

Eleanor sighed and replaced her pen in its casing. "Charles is merely relating how he and Georgianna pass their time together until I return."

Iris regarded her cousin with a look of utter confusion. "But—but, Eleanor! In his letter he speaks of nothing but *her!*"

"Then I must be grateful that Georgianna is so diligent in her duties. Now please, Iris, do let me finish this letter to Charles. If I do not have it ready for the King's Post today, Charles shall not receive it in time and he shall be greatly disappointed."

Iris obliged by picking up a book and moving from the desk to a nearby chair. She made a great show of flipping through the pages of the novel, but she continued to regard Eleanor with an expression of troubled confusion.

Eleanor was too concerned with finishing her letter to notice. Difficult indeed did she find the task of writing to Charles of her deep commitment to him when Iris's words regarding Sir Andrew continued to echo through her mind.

She tried to tell herself that Iris was mistaken, that her cousin was too young and unsophisticated to understand the particular friendship she shared with Andrew. Yet there was no denying the fact that during the past weeks, Andrew had accorded her his unfailing attention; nor could she deny the way her heart skipped a little faster whenever he looked down at her in that quizzing way of his.

She had reason to believe that Andrew derived a certain enjoyment from their friendship as well, or he wouldn't be dancing such close attendance upon her; but she dared not think that his were the actions of a man who was anything more than a friend. He had, after all, made it most clear that he had no intention of offering for her, and that promise, when she chanced to think of it, had the curious effect of sinking her spirits.

Eleanor finished writing her letter to Charles with an effort, penning the last lines while under the influence of a deep sense of guilt for having betrayed Charles.

She was just setting the seal in place when a groom appeared with the dual purpose of collecting the letter for the post and advising her that Sir Andrew de Ardescote was awaiting her pleasure in the main salon downstairs.

Eleanor briefly entertained the notion of sending him away with a message that she was indisposed and unable to drive out with him as they had planned. Yet the prospect of seeing Andrew again was too great to be denied. In her room she quickly donned pelisse, bonnet, and gloves, and presented herself downstairs within a respectable period of time.

Andrew's dark eyes swept over her appreciatively. She was wearing the same pale blue bonnet she had worn the first time he had taken her up in his carriage. With her gold hair shining in the sunlight and her eyes as clear and bright as a country sky, he knew Eleanor for the very picture of loveliness.

He handed her up into the carriage, then stood back and watched for a moment as she arranged her skirts about her, folded her hands in her lap, and then looked straight ahead in a very distracted sort of way.

A faint smile played at the corner of Andrew's mouth.

Here was a new Lady Eleanor Chilton he had not before encountered. Gone were all traces of the very self-assured young lady he usually took up in his curricle. Instead, she sat before him looking quite preoccupied and more than a little lost.

He watched as Eleanor recalled her surroundings with a start and looked down at him in a confused manner he did not find at all unattractive.

"Why do we wait? Are we not driving out to the Gardens?" she asked.

"Indeed we are," replied Andrew, climbing up into the curricle beside her. He drew on his driving gloves and took up his whip, and they were off, touring the streets of London in a now-familiar routine.

Eleanor watched Andrew tool his horses through the traffic with an expertise that was the envy of every man who aspired to the Corinthian set. His long fingers gripped the reins comfortably and he seemed very much at his ease; as calm and contented as one would expect of a man with plans to spend an afternoon strolling through the Botanic Gardens.

Eleanor's emotional state, on the other hand, was not quite as tranquil. In the small confines of the curricle, she sat so close to Andrew that several times his strong arm brushed against her shoulder and sent a fluttering sensation through her; and when he chanced to look down at her, in that quizzing way, and smiled slightly, she was struck by how handsome he really was. She was powerless to fight back the two high spots of color that mantled her cheeks, just as she was powerless to avert her thoughts from the way her every sensation seemed to be attuned to him.

She tried to focus on her hands, rigidly clasped

together in her lap, instead of the feeling of utter guilt that threatened to encompass her. For the briefest of moments she regretted ever coming to London and considered how much simpler her life would be if she had stayed in the country where she belonged. Without a London Season she might by now have been safely and comfortably married to Charles, and might never have met Andrew nor known how quickly her heart might be set to fluttering by the mere nearness of a man.

She had a sudden notion that the cause behind her present heartache could be directly attributed to her father and his horrid scheme to have her presented at court. At his feet did she lay the blame for the present confusion in her heart, and she dearly wished he were with her now that she might rail against him.

But she also wished he could be with her now to lend his shoulder for comfort. Since childhood, Eleanor had found her affectionate father to be a close and trusted confidant; and she held little doubt that he would know just how to advise her in her present circumstance. She needed his wisdom and easy air of confidence to help her sort through her conflicting emotions. Certainly, her papa would be able to explain how a young lady might find herself in the dubious predicament of being betrothed to one gentleman at the same time she was well on her way to losing her heart to another.

A stolen glance at Andrew was enough to convince her that he was not laboring under any similar emotions where she was concerned. Instead, he seemed quite content to do nothing more than view the passing countryside as they entered the gates to the Gardens.

"I am convinced you shall enjoy your tour of the

Gardens much more on foot," Andrew said, alighting gracefully from the carriage and reaching up to clasp her about her slim waist. He swung her down without effort, then tucked her hand in the crook of his arm and led her across the grass, away from his curricle and attending groom.

They strolled together in silence for a short time while Andrew debated how best to proceed. There was an elusive quality to her disposition on this particular afternoon that only served to excite the hunter's instinct within him.

He thought it might be amusing to see if he could tease her out of her melancholy, and he said in his deep voice, "It is a fine afternoon, is it not, Lady Eleanor? Warm, yet not overly so, and the sun shines down so brightly."

These words distracted Eleanor from the preoccupying thoughts that had been troubling her. "Oh! Oh, yes, indeed! The day is very fine," she answered, knowing that some reply was expected and being unable to devise a more clever response.

Andrew brought her to a stop beside him and looked down upon her with one dark brow flying at a familiar angle. "I had thought us well enough acquainted that we need not resort to mundane discussions of the weather."

It was not in her power to resist his charm when he looked down at her in just that way. She smiled slightly as she strove to offer a plausible explanation for her uncommon behavior. "You are right, of course. I—I was merely distracted. The gardens are so lovely. They remind me very much of home, and I'm afraid I am a bit lonesome for my beloved Dessborough Place."

They began walking once again. Andrew's large hand covered Eleanor's smaller one as it rested in the crook of his arm. "And what is it you miss so much about your home?" he asked genially. "Your horses, perhaps, or the mere comfort of having familiar possessions about you? Or perhaps it is the people from your home you miss most?"

She nodded slightly, believing most fervently that she wanted nothing more than to confide to her papa of the inexplicable change in her feelings regarding her marriage to Charles.

"There is only one person I am longing to see," she said quietly, focusing her attention with an effort on the lovely blooms displayed in the gardens.

Andrew did not speak again until they had walked for some time and then his words were clipped as he asked, "I suppose you are speaking of one particular person for whom you care very deeply? Shall I guess as well that person returns your affection?"

She didn't answer with words, but there was no mistaking the definite bounce of her beribboned bonnet as she nodded her head in response.

The firm line of Andrew's lips tightened. So, she was pining for her neighborhood puppy, was she? That same feeling of unreasonable anger crept insidiously to the fore as he continued to lead her through the gardens.

Outwardly, he remained unfailingly courteous; inwardly his resentment simmered, and it wasn't until Eleanor looked up at him with an expression mixed of curiosity, confusion, and discomfort that he realized he was not performing with as much control as he had believed.

She stopped walking and tugged slightly at her hand,

still covered by Andrew's long fingers and cradled in the crook of his arm. "Sir, you're crushing my fingers."

He looked down upon her and she saw immediately that telltale glitter in his eyes that signaled his displeasure. But there was something else that smoldered there, a mysterious light that defied definition and sent a trill of alarm down her spine.

He loosened his grip on her fingers at the same time his attention focused on her softly parted lips. Of a sudden he knew an overwhelming desire to crush her against him and kiss her until all thoughts of Charles Adair were banished forever from her mind. It took every bit of restraint he possessed to fight back the notion and to resume their stroll about the gardens with an air of unconcern. He was not as successful in this vein as he imagined.

As Eleanor walked beside him, she was immediately aware that his movements were far from those of his habitual grace. It seemed, in fact, that he was holding his entire body in check, as if he were controlling himself with an effort.

There was a tension now between them that seemed to have been building from the moment they had set out on their day's excursion, and Eleanor guessed that she was the cause of it.

When Andrew had looked down upon her, his dark eyes lit mysteriously in a manner that had left her breathless, she had wanted nothing more than for him to take her in his arms and kiss her.

That realization left her shaken. Betrothed to the faithful friend of her childhood, she had, for the briefest of moments, been quite willing to return the kisses of another man.

Blessedly, the wide brim of her bonnet served to mask the blushes that mantled her cheeks whenever she chanced to think of her own boldness and her horrid willingness to betray the trust Charles had placed in her.

And she thought of it often, for she realized, with a good deal of turmoil, that she desired nothing more than to be kissed by Sir Andrew de Ardescote.

Chapter Eleven

The Dowager Duchess of Seldon had positioned herself at the head of the stairs in order to greet her guests. Her face, always powdered and painted in a desperate attempt to hide the evidence of her advanced years, was frozen in a smile of much-practiced graciousness. She leaned heavily upon her gilt cane, and wavered slightly from time to time as the *creme de society* passed before her on their way to her conservatory.

At the sight of Lady Glower, she extended one wrinkled, arthritic hand. "So good of you to come, my *dear* Lady Glower!" she said in a quaveringly effusive voice. "And I see you have brought your lovely girls with you! How *splendid!*"

Lady Glower was rather awed by the luxury of her surroundings and the chance to be included among the Duchess's circle of intimates, but she managed to properly introduce her daughter and niece to Her Grace.

The Duchess turned her attention toward Eleanor and Iris and favored them with a surprisingly sharp assessment. "Charming. Quite charming," she pronounced them after a moment's examination.

The girls dropped demure curtsies under their hostess's approving eye, then followed Lady Glower up the grand staircase and down a series of passages.

Iris could barely contain herself over the prospect of being among the guests at one of Her Grace's most exclusive musicales. As they traveled down one particular hallway, her eyes widened at the sight of the many treasures and fineries on display.

"Goodness, Cousin! Have you ever seen anything such as this?" she asked in an exaggerated whisper. "Such finery! I am *quite* overwhelmed!"

Eleanor listened to her cousin's excited patter and wished she might catch a bit of Iris's enthusiasm. Her wishes, however, were to no avail.

Her spirits were dismally low and nothing, not even a much coveted invitation to one of the Duchess of Seldon's lavish musicales, could tempt her from the melancholy mood that enveloped her.

It had been four days since last she had seen Andrew; four long and lonely days in which she had done little else but think of him and wonder what might have occurred that should cause him to so studiously avoid her company.

As she followed Iris and Lady Glower into the conservatory, however, the magnificence of the room caused her to momentarily forget her troubles. The conservatory at Seldon House was a vast room of seemingly endless proportions, alight with the glow of hundreds of candles reflecting off the cut glass chandeliers and column sconces.

At the far end of the room, a small orchestra sat against a backdrop of gracefully arched, multipaned windows that reached from floor to ceiling. They were playing a rather lovely piece of music that could barely be heard over the noise of the assembled guests.

The room was crowded with the most elegantly dressed people Eleanor had yet seen. Chairs aligned in neat rows down the center of the room were already taken and many more guests, engaged in sparkling conversation, milled about the columned walkways on either side of the room.

Eleanor quickly scanned the crowd, hoping to catch a glimpse of Andrew, but she failed to see his tall, muscular figure towering above the crush of people.

Lady Glower was about to bravely lead her charges into the daunting throng of humanity, when Lord Trowbridge stepped before them. He greeted them with characteristic civility, saying, "How do you do? Have you ever seen anything like it? If you've a mind to listen to the music, you shall have to cut a path to the orchestra on the other side of the room—if you're able! The Duchess does like to pack it tight!"

"There *are* a great many people here," allowed Lady Glower. "If you tell me the music is exceptional, I shall try to make my way to it."

"Oh, one fugue is very much like another to me," said Lord Trowbridge, candidly. "I shouldn't make too great an effort to hear it, if it means suffering the odd elbow in one's side or running the risk of having a glass of champagne emptied on one's trouser leg."

"That settles it! We shall remain quite comfortably

at this end of the room!'' said Lady Glower, with relief. ''If I am not mistaken, I spied my dear friend, Mrs. Brandon-Howe, by that first pillar, and I believe I may make my way to her if I am persistent.''

Lady Glower set off toward her friend with Iris in tow, while Eleanor remained behind with Lord Trowbridge.

''What do you think of all this, Lady Eleanor?'' he asked amiably.

Her blue eyes scanned the room with interest. ''It's all quite dazzling, isn't it? I was quite captivated when we first arrived, but now I must admit the noise is a bit overwhelming.''

''Just wait until you've been here another ten minutes or so and you'll begin to feel the heat this kind of jam generates. It's considered quite *de rigueur* for society's finest ladies to faint dead away at one of the Duchess's musicales. I believe the old lady relies upon at least two fainting spells per evening or she doesn't consider the party a success.''

Eleanor couldn't help but laugh. ''In that case, I do not wish to be at all fashionable! Do you suppose there is somewhere one might find a bit of fresh air?''

Lord Trowbridge smiled. ''There is indeed. Let me show you!'' He offered Eleanor his arm and led her through the throng of people to a side door that opened onto a hallway, off of which were various salons.

Their exit would have drawn little attention, except for the fact that Sir Andrew and Captain Lisle entered the conservatory just in time to see Eleanor disappear from view on the arm of Lord Trowbridge.

Captain Lisle drew nearer his friend in an effort to be heard over the noise of the guests and said, ''I say,

Drew, wasn't that Eleanor with Trowbridge, just now? Where could they be going, do you suppose?"

"I don't know," said Andrew, through suddenly clenched teeth, "but I'm damn well going to find out."

He had, in fact, no idea why Eleanor and Lord Trowbridge might have left the assembly together. He knew only that he resented seeing them do so. No amount of reasoning could persuade him that some bit of logic might explain their leaving the crowded gathering; instead, he chose to dwell upon the notion that they had gone in search of another, more intimate spot where they might find themselves quite alone. The thought made him frankly furious.

For four long days Andrew had studiously avoided Eleanor's company. He had wanted to prove to himself that he could pass an agreeable day without seeing her lovely face smiling up at him. He had discovered that he could not. He had missed seeing her and had foolishly hoped that she might have missed him. He knew now that she had not missed him or she wouldn't have been quite so quick to arrange a tête-á-tête with Lord Trowbridge.

He began making his way through the guests with Captain Lisle close behind. His progress was slow, impeded by a number of people who wished to exchange greetings with him or capture his attention for the briefest of moments. By the time he was finally able to quit the conservatory, Andrew's temper was in full career.

He inspected several rooms before he finally walked into a small salon to find Eleanor. She was not, however, in the arms of Lord Trowbridge, as he might have expected. Instead, it was Lord Montfort who stood with one hand about her slim waist, while his other hand tried to capture Eleanor's chin, the better to hold her still so he might kiss her.

Eleanor, a look of patent alarm on her face, fought vainly against captor. "No! No, please let me go! Oh, don't just stand there, Lord Trowbridge! Please help me!" But young Lord Trowbridge, who a mere moment before had been quite content to play a part in ensuring that his good friend Montfort at last claimed a kiss from Lady Eleanor and won that long-outstanding bet, now stood quite frozen at the sight of Sir Andrew de Ardescote's face, gone dark with thunderous anger.

"Montfort, I've a mind to teach you some manners," said Andrew in a quietly ominous voice that effectively captured Lord Montfort's attention.

His lordship immediately released Eleanor to find Andrew descending upon him, his face a mask of fury and his fists clenched in warning.

"Here now, de Ardescote, you can't mean to pelt me over Lady Chill!" Montfort weakly protested, backing away with an arm raised in defense. "Only trying to get a leg up on you. After all, the deadline *is* drawing near. Damme, you would have done the same in my position!"

It was an uncommon occurrence for Sir Andrew de Ardescote, the Fashionable Corinthian, to so completely lose the mastery of himself; but an almost blind fury seized him at the very thought that a man of Montfort's stamp might force himself upon Eleanor. One of his large fists, long cocked and ready, coiled back as a prelude to striking his lordship.

"Don't do it, Drew," recommended Captain Lisle, capturing in midair Andrew's poised fist. "You can't send Montfort back into the Duchess's conservatory with his claret drawn!''

Andrew made a move to wrest his arm loose, but the Captain refused to free him. ''No, dash it, I won't let you! Think, man! Starting a brawl at a *ton* assembly is a blight even *your* consequence won't overcome! If nothing else, think of the damage such a story shall do Eleanor!''

For the first time since entering the salon, Andrew spared more than a fleeting glance toward Eleanor. He had been so intent on pummeling her attacker that he had failed to notice how pale she was or that the shock of Lord Montfort's advances had left her rather weak and trembling. Her blue eyes were wide as she regarded him, and he had a notion that she was bravely fighting back tears. He had never seen her more lovely and he had every intention of taking her in his arms and holding her until all thoughts of the treatment she had suffered at the hand of that cur, Montfort, were forever banished from her mind.

''You shall oblige me, Montfort, by leaving the room,'' said Andrew, his eyes never leaving Eleanor's stricken face.

His lordship, fully aware that he had narrowly escaped the brunt of de Ardescote's legendary wrath, did not need to be asked twice. He moved quickly across the room, his friend, Lord Trowbridge, fast following, when Andrew's deep, burning voice brought him to a halt.

''And, Montfort, you would be wise to ensure that your path never again crosses mine.''

His lordship's face colored alarmingly with a characteristic burst of sudden emotion; but he quickly weighed the consequence of fanning Andrew's temper to new and possibly uncontrollable heights, and he left the room without a word.

"I had better follow to ensure they quit the house altogether without talking to anyone," said Captain Lisle. Andrew barely waited for his friend to leave the room before he stepped toward Eleanor. His simple gesture was all the invitation she required, and she rushed into the comfort of his open arms.

For a long while he merely held her, reveling in the feel of her pliant body against his and breathing deeply of the sweet fragrance of her golden curls as they danced against his chin.

"Eleanor, my darling, did that bounder hurt you?" he asked at last.

"I—I don't think so," she replied, her voice muffled against his shirt front. "But he was so determined to kiss me, and I was equally determined that he should not!"

"Had you and Montfort been engaged in a battle of wills, I have no doubt you would have emerged the victor. However determined you may be, you are no match for a man of Montfort's strength and monstrous plans."

"I can only thank you for arriving when you did," said Eleanor raising her eyes, bright with gratitude, toward his. "It has been so long since I have seen you. What an odious bit of luck that we should at last meet again, under such an embarrassing circumstance! Yet, I must say that there is no one else I should rather have come to my rescue. I—I don't know how I may ever show my gratitude!"

Andrew looked down at the young woman he held in his arms and formed a fairly good notion of what form he would like to see her gratitude expressed. "It wasn't luck that brought me to this room. I saw you leave the conservatory with Trowbridge," said Andrew, neatly failing to mention the spark of jealousy that had caused him to go in search of her in the first place. He looked down at her with a suddenly stern expression. "Eleanor, you must not go off alone with a man in future."

"No? Not even if the man is you?"

Andrew's eyes briefly scanned her upturned face as he tightened his arms about her. *"Especially* if the man is me."

Chapter Twelve

Eleanor felt Andrew's arms tighten about her and felt her own heart quicken in response. The movement of his long fingers about her waist and shoulders sent a wave of unfamiliar sensations dancing through her. She felt a little breathless and light-headed as her head tipped back against his shoulder and she gazed up into his face.

His expression was unreadable. She saw no discernible emotion in his handsome features. Only a throbbing pulse in the column of his muscled neck told her that his cool control was at risk.

Her gaze traveled to his lips. In that moment she wanted nothing more than for Andrew to kiss her. Surely he must care for her, she reasoned, or his strong hands wouldn't gently press her so against his powerful body. Surely that curious warmth that was suddenly flickering within her was fanning to life within him, as well.

But he didn't kiss her. Instead, his arms suddenly

went rigid about her and before Eleanor's eyes, his expression altered rapidly to one of disbelief, as if some unexpected realization had left him startled and shaken.

He stared down at her with now-hardened features that sent a small thrill of alarm through Eleanor. She took a step back, and he released her with an ease she found wholly disappointing. Apparently, Andrew had not enjoyed their brief embrace. He looked down upon her with an almost insulting composure. She, on the other hand, was forced to make a concerted effort to remain standing on legs that suddenly felt like a substance curiously resembling blancmange.

Wholly bewildered, Eleanor could only stare at him, unable to credit that such rigid, impassive features could truly belong to the same man who had looked upon her with tenderness but moments before.

They stood regarding each other in uncertain silence when the door opened and Captain Lisle entered. He said, with a good deal of satisfaction, "Well, I've seen Montfort and Trowbridge out! I should think, Lady Eleanor, you shall have no more to fear from their barbarous behavior!"

His ready smile faded rapidly as he looked from Andrew to Eleanor and back to Andrew again. "Have—have I intruded? I—I beg your pardon!"

"Nonsense," said Andrew in a voice that was far from reassuring. "As it happens, I was just about to rejoin the party. And as you have proved yourself particularly adept at playing the escort, Lisle, perhaps you will be good enough to return Lady Eleanor to the conservatory when she is ready?"

He spoke in a cool, dispassionate tone; then he executed a brief, rather curt bow and left the room without so much as a glance toward Eleanor.

Stunned, she turned toward Captain Lisle as if he might be able to offer some explanation for his friend's uncommon behavior, but no words came to her. She could only stand there, mute, wishing with all her heart that Andrew would return and fold her into his comforting embrace as he had when first he had entered the salon.

Captain Lisle shifted uncomfortably as he saw Eleanor's eyes fill with sudden tears. "Here, now, Lady Eleanor! Please don't cry, of all things!"

But it was too late, for Eleanor was unable to check the tears that fell in glistening paths down her pale cheeks. She turned beseeching eyes upon him and said in a pathetic, small voice, "I don't understand him at all! They say women are difficult to know, but he is of all men the most perplexing creature I have ever met!"

Captain Lisle was rather inclined to agree with this assessment of his friend, but thought better than to say so. Instead, he produced a large kerchief from his pocket and offered it to Eleanor. "Yes, well, Drew is cut from a different cloth than the rest of us when it comes to a great many things." He had a sudden thought and asked, rather warily, "He—he didn't come the ugly with you just now, did he? I've never known him to be anything but a perfect gentleman where a lady is concerned."

Eleanor directed her watery gaze to the kerchief that was being worked into a worried knot between her fingers. "That, I believe, is the very problem! I—I thought he would kiss me, you see, for he was holding me and looking at me as if he should very much like to. But he did not and I wanted very much for him to do so but—oh, Captain Lisle, I am so unhappy!''

Captain Lisle watched in alarm as a fresh tide of tears coursed down her cheeks. ''Lady Eleanor, you mustn't! I beg you won't cry or I shall be quite disarmed! Besides, you must know that you are wrong about Drew. I know for a fact that he very much *wants* to kiss you!''

''Are you quite sure?'' asked Eleanor, emerging from behind the kerchief.

''Pon my honor.''

''Then why didn't he do so when he had the opportunity?''

The Captain looked puzzled. ''Had the opportunity? Do you mean you might have let him kiss you and he declined?''

''I should *gladly* have allowed him to kiss me,'' said Eleanor in a voice of passion.

Captain Lisle stared at her a moment, then said in a wondrous tone, ''Well, damme, I shouldn't have thought it.''

''What do you mean?'' demanded Eleanor, immediately distressed. ''Do you mean he did *not* want to kiss me?''

''No, no! Nothing of the kind,'' he quickly assured her. ''I am convinced that his feelings for you are— Well, I shouldn't be saying so! But clearly he did not kiss you because it is a matter of chivalry with him.''

Eleanor looked at him sadly, the threat of fresh tears gathering in her blue eyes. ''Because I am betrothed to another? Do you mean he cannot care for me because he believes my heart is already taken?''

Captain Lisle, clearly distressed by the task of comforting a weeping woman, rushed to correct her. "Upon my word, that is not the reason!"

Eleanor squared her slim shoulders and dabbed at her eyes with the damp kerchief. "You have been very kind to me, Captain, and I shall not distress you any further with my tears. I wish with all my heart that I might believe you when you tell me Andrew cares for me, but I fear I cannot!"

This show of bravado threw him off his stride much more effectively than her tears ever did. He seized her hand in a pleading grip and begged, "What can I say to convince you of Andrew's feelings? How can I assure you that he would gladly kiss you, if for no other reason than to win the bet with—"

Captain Lisle stopped short, painfully aware that he was guilty of a gross indiscretion. He offered up a silent prayer that Eleanor should not seize upon his hasty words but one look at her face with her fine brows raised in a questioning manner, was enough to convince him that his unfortunate words had not gone unnoticed.

"Win the bet?" repeated Eleanor. "What bet is that, Captain Lisle?"

He met her inquisitive gaze with confusion. "Bet? Well, I—I am not quite sure. Men do wager all the time and over the most trifling of things! I shouldn't refine too much upon it, if I were you, for it's very likely forgotten!"

"But what does kissing me have to do with a bet men should make?" insisted Eleanor.

"I—I'm not entirely certain," he answered weakly.

"Was Andrew involved in the wager? With whom did he bet?"

Captain Lisle's eyes scanned the room as if seeking

out possible avenues of escape as he silently cursed his friend for having left him in such a situation. "Oh, I— I don't believe I recall any names!"

"I think you are being deliberately provocative," said Eleanor with a flash of impatience, "and I have never spent a more trying evening! You tell me that Andrew should kiss me because of a bet. But what, I ask you, has that to say to me? All I know is that I *want* Andrew to kiss me, and he will not. On the other hand, I did not want Lord Montfort to kiss me and he was most willing! What nonsense is this?"

She recognized the expression of utter misery on Captain Lisle's face at the very instant she recognized the importance of her own words. "You—you did say that Andrew had to—to kiss me to win a bet," she stammered, her wide, horrified eyes begging him deny the notion that was fast forming in her mind. "Was that the wager? That he should kiss me before Lord Montfort did?"

Captain Lisle was unable to counter her accusing tone. As it happened, there was no need, for in his wretched expression did Eleanor have her answer. For a moment she was stunned, but that fleeting emotion was quickly replaced by anger and a mounting sense of injury.

"So! Andrew and Lord Montfort made a shameless wager to see who should kiss me first, did they? And how, pray, was I selected as the fortunate damsel who should receive such honor as this?"

Captain Lisle swallowed hard. "Well, I—I'm not entirely certain. That is—I shouldn't refine too much upon this ghastly business, if I were you!"

He watched as Eleanor drew her delicate frame up

to a determined height. Blue eyes sparking and cheeks becomingly flushed, she appeared quite ready to do battle and win. All signs pointed toward an emotional scene about to erupt and he steeled himself against it.

He was glad to discover that Eleanor was made of much sterner stuff than he had imagined. No tears came; no biting recriminations escaped her soft lips. Only that militant spark flashed within the depths of her clear, blue eyes. Had he been better acquainted with her, he might have begged her to consider that whenever she was in the throes of such emotion, she tended to behave in a rash and unpredictable manner. Instead, he could only be glad that her tears had dried up and she appeared very much in control of herself.

Her voice was oddly calm as she said, "Dear Captain Lisle, will you grant me one favor? Will you be good enough to escort me back to my aunt?"

He could not have been more relieved. "Is that all? I should say so, Lady Eleanor! May I take you now? Here, do take my arm!" he invited, solicitously drawing her to her feet and leading her across the room toward the door. "I must say, you're taking this all very well. Game as a pebble and plenty of pluck! You're doing the right thing to put this entire ghastly business out of your mind."

Eleanor forced a smile to her lips as she preceded the Captain out into the hallway. Throughout the remainder of the evening, her lovely face wore that vague and distantly polite expression; and in so doing, she fit quite well among the other guests crushed into the confines of the music room.

The noise of the assembled guests and the orchestra made conversation quite impossible for anyone. Eleanor, with her lips schooled into that hint of a smile, stood amid the crowd of people quite undisturbed and gave herself up to plotting the success of her most pressing desire: To punish somehow Sir Andrew de Ardescote beyond any possibility of his recovery.

Chapter Thirteen

Captain Lisle turned his mount down the stretch of tan that followed the carriage path and resumed his search for Andrew. There were few riders in Hyde Park at this particular hour of the morning and he allowed his horse to break into a gallop. He hoped, with a fervor born of desperation, that he would find his friend in good time.

He was to have his wish. He spotted Andrew riding near the South Gate and gave a shout that effectively caught Andrew's attention.

"By all that's wonderful, I've found you at last!" exclaimed the Captain in a breathless manner as he reined in alongside his friend.

Andrew cast him a bland look, controlling his horse with little effort as it sidled and fidgeted and tossed its head. "You're glaringly abroad this morning, Lisle. Who gave you leave to ride in that neck-or-nothing fashion in the Park?"

"Never mind that!" the Captain retorted, catching his breath. "Did your man tell you that I came round last night, demanding to see you? The cursed fellow turned me out! No matter what argument I put forth, he refused to admit me!"

"Yes, I know," said Andrew, easily. "I told him to send you away."

Captain Lisle stiffened. "*You*? Why did you do that?"

Andrew shrugged his great shoulders. "I thought you were on the toodle and looking for someone to join your plunge into the cups."

"But I—I wasn't!" sputtered the Captain.

"My mistake, then," said Andrew simply.

"But I came to you on a matter of great import!"

"Important enough that I should be called from my bed at three o'clock in the morning? Then it *was* my mistake. Tell me, is the matter still of such urgency? Shall it be worth your while to speak of it now?"

"I should say so!" retorted Captain Lisle, who could not help but add, with a burning look, "and once you've heard the whole of it, I shouldn't doubt you'll regret not hearing me out when I came to you the first time!"

Andrew glanced down at him from his superior height and debated for a moment whether his friend's reproach was worthy of a reply. He decided it was not.

He had spent a most trying night. Sleep had eluded him for hours as visions of Eleanor, in one form or another, had danced before his eyes. His thoughts were full of her and the manner in which she had melded so easily into his arms. It took little effort on his part to conjure a memory of her soft, pink lips raised invitingly toward his. Still less effort did it take to recall how natural it had seemed to fold her delicately curved body within the strong circle of his embrace.

His desire to kiss her had been overwhelming. She belonged in his arms. She belonged to him; and for a few brief moments he was able to forget everything— their surroundings, even her betrothal to another man. He knew only that he wanted to hold her in his arms forever and kiss her until she begged him to stop. And then he would kiss her some more.

How the memory of that cursed bet had managed to intrude upon such sensuous thoughts, he truly had no idea; but his sudden recollection of the wager had surfaced at the exact moment he had realized an overwhelming need to possess her.

A frustrated note of annoyance escaped his lips as he suddenly turned his spirited horse down the track and allowed it to break into a canter.

"Hold up now, Drew! You must hear me out!" cried the Captain.

Andrew rode on, quite intent on ignoring that note of urgency in his friend's tone; but his attention was effectively caught when he heard the Captain call after him, "Andrew! I've come about Eleanor!"

He reined in quickly and turned his mount back to cover the distance between them with surprising speed. Abreast of the Captain, he looked down upon him with a dark expression, that telltale glitter creeping into the depths of his eyes, and demanded in a thunderously low voice, "What have you to say of Eleanor?"

Captain Lisle swallowed hard, unsure if he possessed the courage to proceed. Gladly would he have faced an entire regiment of Napoleon's forces single-handedly rather than confess his conversation with Eleanor and endure Andrew's wrath. "She was quite distraught last night! Couldn't make sense of the fact that you didn't kiss her when you had the opportunity."

A telltale pulse throbbed within the column of Andrew's neck. "I can well imagine," he said, dryly. "I am having some difficulty in making sense of it myself."

"But don't you see? She *wanted* you to kiss her!"

Andrew looked at him sharply. "How do you know this?"

"Told me so. She was in a rare state, I can tell you! Said she would *gladly* have let you kiss her right then and there! She couldn't understand why you didn't kiss her and—and, frankly, I can't understand it myself!"

"Can't you?" asked Andrew, darkly.

"No! No, I can't," said the Captain, with sudden courage. "I know you care for her. I've seen how you are whenever she's near you. And, even more telling, I've seen how you are when she's *not* about. So why, then, would you not kiss the woman you love and win a tidy sum besides?"

Andrew turned his darkly glittering gaze upon his friend. "Damn the wager!" he said, with a violence of feeling. "I wish to God I had never met with Montfort that night, nor embarked upon that wretched bet!"

"It's remedied easily enough. Simply kiss her. Kiss her and be done with the entire business."

Andrew almost groaned in response. "That, my friend, is the one thing I cannot do. To kiss Eleanor now would prove a grave mistake. To kiss her, knowing full well that my fortune and reputation in the clubs of St. James would profit by it, is something I cannot bring myself to do."

Indeed, denying himself that kiss had been one of

the most difficult things he had ever done. Even now he could recall with stunning clarity the manner in which Eleanor's slim, pliant body had felt against his. The unfulfilled promise of her soft lips, ready to be kissed, left his temper far from improved.

"There must be a way to extricate myself from that cursed wager," he muttered.

"Then I've the answer," said Captain Lisle. "Leave the field to Montfort. Once the wager is settled, you need have no scruples regarding Eleanor. Then you may court her in earnest."

Andrew stared at him with a look of appalled horror. "Let Montfort kiss Eleanor? Never! Good God, man! Have you taken leave of your senses?"

"Then, what *will* you do?"

"There's nothing for it, but to confess the whole to her," said Andrew in a quiet voice.

Captain Lisle squirmed uneasily. "Here, now. Perhaps that is not such a splendid idea. Perhaps—perhaps she already knows of the wager."

"And how in blue blazes would she know anything about it?"

Captain Lisle cleared his throat and debated the relative merits of confession and of having a clear conscience. He cleared his throat again and plunged: "Well, you know, she's such a fragile-looking, little thing. She was quite distressed last night and—well, when she started to cry, yet fought so bravely not to, I was quite disarmed, I can tell you!"

This earned him a sudden and fiery glance from Andrew, and he hastened to add, "Of course, you know how she is. Stuck that little chin of hers up in that way she has and behaved for all the world as if she didn't care. Extraordinary woman in that way.''

But Andrew wasn't listening. His thoughts were on Eleanor as he drew a hand across his chin and muttered, ''I shall have to see her and confess everything. Though what I am to say, I have no idea.''

''Say nothing,'' advised the Captain. ''Let the thing run its course. Believe me, she won't know the difference. A quick kiss from Montfort and your way is clear to pursue her and make it all right and tight.''

Frowning, Andrew tried to consider his friend's words. Instead, his thoughts were invaded by memories of Eleanor, standing within his arms. In his heart he knew she wanted that kiss as much as he did; in his heart he knew that while he held her, she never gave that affianced country squire of hers a single thought. He didn't want to risk losing her to some bumpkin that was awaiting her return to Dessborough Place; and he certainly had no intention of allowing Montfort to kiss her. It appeared he had but one avenue available.

''You mistake, Lisle,'' he said, at last. ''I must confess. Either I confess or I find a way to extricate myself from that bet. And since the latter possibility is not to be entertained, given the other party involved, I have no recourse but to confess all and hope she may forgive my beastly behavior.''

Andrew made to move away then, but Captain Lisle's hand shot out to grip the reins in a desperate hold. ''Drew, if you confess the whole of it to Eleanor, there's a chance the entire business will end as unappealing as a dog's dinner! You—you see that I'm right, don't you?''

''If Eleanor were only half as distressed last night as you say, I should guess that of all things, she needs some reassurance from me as to my intentions. I intend to go to her and give her that reassurance—as soon as you have removed your hand from my bridle."

From experience Captain Lisle knew better than to argue when Andrew spoke with just that tone of quiet, careful control. Once more did he entertain the notion of confessing to Andrew that he had told Eleanor of the bet. Once more did his courage fail him and he let loose the reins of Andrew's horse.

Andrew smiled slightly. "Don't look so worried. I promise you, I will have confessed the whole of it and shall have her in my arms before her morning coffee is cold in the cup." He touched his horse and set off down the track at a gallop, headed toward the West Gate and Glower House.

Chapter Fourteen

The shops along Bond Street contained exactly the items which Eleanor needed. Had she been in a more frivolous state of mind, she might have been well pleased with her day's purchases; but she appeared to all who chanced to observe her actions to derive not the least enjoyment from her expedition to that street's exclusive shopping establishments. She appeared instead to be a lady with a purpose as she moved from one shop or display to another in her quest for the exact item of which she was in need.

Lady Glower, rarely intuitive under the best of circumstances, saw nothing amiss in her niece's demeanor. Shopping along Bond Street with her daughter and niece was of all things what she enjoyed most, and she had yet been given no reason to believe otherwise might be true of Eleanor.

She was, instead, quite caught up in the anticipation of the masked ball and had shepherded her daughter and niece to the dressmaker's shop to pick up the cloaks they had ordered to wear for the evening.

"My dearest, how clever you are!" she exclaimed, fingering the pale blue satin material the seamstress had fashioned into a voluminous domino on Eleanor's orders. "Only see how this color shows your eyes to advantage! You shall be quite stunning, my dearest Eleanor. I dare not think any other guest shall appear at Mrs. Beringer's masked ball in a domino of such a delicate shade!"

Eleanor forced a smile that did not quite reach her eyes. "Then I will have accomplished my purpose. Dear aunt, you have discovered me, for it is my plan exactly that my domino of pale blue shall look like no other."

Lady Glower beamed happily upon her niece and daughter. "Such intrigue! I swear I believe I am more eager for this masked ball than either of you girls! And what a stunning entrance we shall make, with Eleanor in this exquisite blue and my Iris gowned in a very lovely lavender." She picked up a bolt of cloth she had been examining for some time and asked, "Iris dear, what do you think of this? I have ordered a new domino made up in this dove gray, yet I am sure my old domino of rose is still quite serviceable. Still, I shall be quite jealous if you and Eleanor are to have such lovely cloaks and I am not allowed one myself! Which do you think I should wear, child?"

From the time they had left the house that morning, Iris Glower's attention had been fixed upon her Cousin Eleanor. She was, frankly, quite worried about her, and had not yet been presented an opportunity to speak with her in private to determine the cause behind her odd manner. But at her mother's question, Iris set aside her concern for Eleanor long enough to summon a bit of enthusiasm. "I think you should not deny yourself the treat of wearing something new. Of course you must wear the gray. Only see how prettily it has been made up! Then together the three of us shall make quite an entrance, indeed!"

Lady Glower smiled delightedly and moved away to examine a length of lace that had caught her attention.

Iris seized the opportunity for a few moments of private conversation with Eleanor and said in a voice that was at once low yet penetrating, "Cousin, I shudder to think what plots may be forming in that head of yours!"

Eleanor started, for she hadn't thought her behavior to have been so noticeable as to incite comment. She continued to finger the pale blue satin and asked, quite casually, "Whatever do you mean?"

"I mean you have got *that* look about you!" hissed Iris. She saw Eleanor turn wide eyes upon her and said, "And pray do not try to play the innocent with me, for you know very well what I am talking about! There is a certain look you get about you when you are hatching a plot of some kind. You had that same look on your face the time we were children and you substituted a full game bag in the pillow cover on Cousin Edwin's bed after he had behaved so abominably to you that afternoon in the park. And consider the time Cousin Cassandra lied to your papa and said you were to blame for the ink stain on the carpet instead of her! You wore the very same look on your face just before Cassandra discovered that all her stockings had been stitched together! A very poor opinion you must have of me, to think I should not know you well enough after all these years!"

Eleanor moved along to another table upon which were displayed several lovely fabrics. She tried to appear unconcerned, as if she were examining each bolt of material with critical eyes; but her eyes were too full of unexpected and equally unwanted tears for her to even be aware of the color of the fabric she held in her gloved hand. It would be impossible, she knew, to confide in Iris; for Iris, ever honest and well behaved, would no doubt feel compelled to relate the whole of Eleanor's scheme to Lady Glower. Then her plan would be quite ruined, and she would be denied the satisfaction of exacting her revenge upon Andrew. That was a risk she was not willing to run.

"Good heavens, Iris, I am a lady now!" she said, with a forced note of cheerfulness. "Are you to throw into my face the things I did as a child? Really, you must not read too much into my demeanor. I am merely tired and longing to rest. I shall be quite set to rights by tomorrow morning, I assure you."

"Stuff!" said Iris, unconvinced. "Oh, I do know you are tired, for I have noticed those circles of sleeplessness under your eyes. But I have also noticed that you seem to be moving about with a certain amount of dull resignation, as if you had seen into the future and found unhappiness there and yourself powerless to change your fate." She hesitated a moment before taking Eleanor's hand and asking with deep concern, "Dearest Cousin, is it Sir Andrew? Have you quarreled with him?"

If only that were so! thought Eleanor, once again fending off the threat of tears. A quarrel was nothing more than a passing blight that could be very easily remedied. Unrequited love, on the other hand, was a virulent plague for which, she was sure, there was no cure.

A strong mixture of emotion brewed within Eleanor. She felt torn between a bruising sense of hurt and the thrilling recollection of being held in Andrew's arms. That she should have discovered Andrew's treachery so close upon the heels of realizing her love for him in the midst of his embrace, had proved to be a cruel trick of fate.

Iris was right. Eleanor *was* merely moving through the paces of the day with a certain amount of dull resignation. Sometime in the early morning hours, as she had lain in bed with sleep dancing just out of reach, she had put the finishing touches to her plan of revenge that would result in the humiliation of Andrew and Lord Montfort.

If all went well, she would have her revenge in full view of the assembled guests at Mrs. Beringer's masked ball. Andrew, she knew, would not suffer such treatment gladly. She had a sudden notion that her last glimpse of Andrew would see him white with fury, staring at her with accusing eyes that glittered ominously.

The success of her plan meant that she would leave London under a cloud, packed aboard the next coach bound for Dessborough Place. Even the thought of returning home brought her no joy. No longer could she entertain the notion of marrying Charles Adair. To marry Charles knowing full well that her heart could never belong to any other but Andrew was something she could not bring herself to do.

The tears came again, and she pulled her hand from Iris's grasp to search her reticule for a kerchief.

"Here, Cousin, take mine," said Iris, handing her a

delicately embroidered bit of muslin. She stood loyally by Eleanor's side until she was certain her cousin was again in command of her emotions. "Dearest Eleanor, you must not be so unhappy. Only think what a fortunate girl you are! Why, you are in the enviable position of having both your childhood friend and the most eligible bachelor in all of London vying for your affections!"

Eleanor sniffed and shook her head sadly. How naive dear Iris was! And how much the real truth of the matter hurt! Eleanor longed to tell Iris how mistaken she was, but her pride would not allow her to admit that Lady Eleanor Chilton had received the attentions of the most eligible man in all of England merely so he might win some odious wager.

Aloud she said, in a rather tragic voice, "I shall never marry! There is nothing left for me but to retire to the country and end my life an old maid. I shall be quite shriveled and unattractive, shunned by Andrew and Charles and all other gentlemen of my acquaintance."

Iris smiled slightly and said in a kinder tone, "Dear Cousin, I don't believe you need end your days in such a fashion, if only you will give up whatever horrid scheme you have set in motion."

Eleanor gave her head a short, determined shake and dabbed at her eyes, as if she were done with all further displays of emotion. "Horrid scheme? Cousin, I am sure I do not know what you may be talking about. But if I *did* hatch such a scheme and if I *were* resolved to see it through, it should be because I have little other choice. It would be because—because I have been deeply hurt and because my pride will not allow the cruelty done me to go unpunished."

Iris was plainly worried. "I cannot help but think that

you shall only make matters worse by insisting upon your revenge. Dear Eleanor, I beg you to reconsider! If Sir Andrew has hurt you in some way, I assure you it was not by design!"

Eleanor gave her a sharp look. "How do you know this? Has he spoken to you?"

"Why, no! Of course not! I am not in his confidence, but to be so is hardly necessary. One has only to watch his expression whenever his eyes light upon you to know his heart is yours!"

Eleanor was far from satisfied by this bit of logic. "I suppose you come by such notions from one of your lending library novels."

"I come by such notions from observing that Sir Andrew never appears happier than when he is with you," said Iris in a soft, low, but somehow compelling voice. "I come by such notions from seeing that he never takes his eyes off you whenever you are in the same room; and by seeing how his attention always wanders back to you whenever he is forced to make conversation with another. *That* is how I come by such notions!"

Eleanor felt the now-familiar prick of tears in the backs of her eyes and once again she fought against them. Her careful self-control was wearing dangerously thin, and for a moment she was quite afraid that she might dissolve into a puddle of tears right in the middle of the shop and under the curious stares of the other patrons.

She collected herself with an effort and said, "I cannot think you know Andrew as I do. Yes, his behavior is quite convincing, but if only you knew the reason behind his attentiveness toward me—oh, Iris, I cannot speak of this, but you must believe me when I tell you his blood is more Borgia than royal!"

"I wonder if you would say such things were he to stand before you now!"

"I should say such and a good deal more," said Eleanor with resolve. "If Andrew de Ardescote has the least suspicion that I know of his cruelty to me, he would do well never to call on me again!"

As it happened Andrew harbored no such suspicions or he might not, at that very moment, have climbed the front steps of Glower House.

He was admitted to the house by Lady Glower's exceptional butler. "Regrettably, the ladies are not at home, sir," said that stately employee, as he bowed Andrew into the front hall. "Shall I tell them you called, sir?"

Andrew handed his coat and hat to a footman and dropped his gloves on a nearby table with a familiarity born of practice. "I shall await their return. In the blue drawing room, I think? No, don't bother showing me. I know my way," he said, and he crossed the hall to climb the wide staircase to the first floor.

Andrew threw open the door to the drawing room, walked in, and shut the door behind him. Only then did he realize that there was another person already in the room.

Chapter Fifteen

In the blue drawing room of Glower House, a young man was engaged in rehearsing a rather impassioned speech to the empty room. At Andrew's entrance he jerked round his head and sprang to his feet. His cheeks colored as Andrew regarded him with unmasked curiosity.

"How do you do?" asked Andrew. "I hope you don't object to an audience."

"Sir!" exclaimed the young man, his cheeks flushing. "I—I had thought myself alone!"

"And so you shall be, as soon as you vacate this room," replied Andrew, smoothly.

Startled, the young man colored more deeply and sputtered, rather defensively, "I—I await Lady Eleanor's return! I have traveled all night to be here and—and I shall not return to Dessborough until I have seen her!"

Andrew's dark brow cocked at this and he regarded

the young man with renewed interest. Dessborough? Could *this* be Eleanor's country squire?

He gave the young man a closer look. Charles Adair was all fancy waistcoat, tall cane, and fob; an unpolished mushroom by London standards who, in the country, was undoubtedly considered quite the sprig of fashion.

A strong and sudden desire to discover the reason for Mr. Adair's visit seized him and he said, in a more amiable tone, "Then perhaps we might wait together. You see, I, too, have called to see Lady Eleanor."

Charles stared at him with unabashed surprise. "You? I—I had no idea you were acquainted with Eleanor!"

"Then you know who I am?"

"To be sure, I do!" said Charles, admiringly. "I should have to be burned to the socket not to recognize the Fashionable Corinthian! I saw your likeness once in *Sporting Magazine* with an account of how you took the field at Heythrop. And last year, when my father came to London to take care of some sort of business, he brought me with him and we saw you in the crowd at a fisticuff bout at Fives Court! It—it is an honor, indeed, to meet you, sir!"

"Very flattering," said Andrew, as he crossed to a side table on which reposed a decanter of Madeira and some glasses. "Now, allow me to return the compliment for I know who you are, as well. Here, take this," he said, pouring out a glass of the wine and handing it to Charles. "I've a feeling you're going to need it."

"You—you know *me*?" asked Charles, going pink with pleasure and surprise.

"Eleanor has mentioned you often enough. I understand you are to be married."

"Oh! Oh, yes! Yes, I am," stammered Charles, his ready smile fading rapidly.

"You may count yourself lucky. There are any number of men who would gladly take your place. Lady Eleanor is the most sought-after beauty of the Season."

Charles cast him an incredulous stare. "Eleanor? You're bamming me! Oh, I beg your pardon!" he rushed, seeing Andrew's disapproving brow cock his direction. "It's only that Eleanor has mentioned nothing of this in any of her letters. In fact, I should have thought her utterly miserable and without a friend in the world, judging from the volumes of complaints she's been sending me over the last two months' time!"

"Is that why you've come to London, then? To see for yourself her situation and whisk her back to the protective embrace of Dessborough, if need be?"

"Good lord, no!" exclaimed Charles, a good deal alarmed by the suggestion. "Eleanor is very well able to take care of herself! I'm here to speak to her of another matter."

"Ah, you must be referring to your betrothal," said Andrew with unnerving accuracy.

"Yes, well—if the truth were known, you would see for yourself that we're not really betrothed, at all," said Charles in the manner of a man who was about to explain away a pesky annoyance. He took a fortifying drink of Madeira. "You see, there have been no banns. No announcement. More of an understanding, is all. Oh, we talked about going ahead with the business, but nothing promised! No, that's not true, for I did promise, but—but not *really!*" He cast Andrew a look of appeal. "*You* know how it is!"

Andrew crossed to the mantelpiece and leaned

against it, as if completely at his leisure; but the glittering lights had begun to dance within the depths of his dark eyes and he fixed Charles with an unwavering stare. He said, silkily, "No, I'm afraid I *don't* know. Tell me."

Charles tossed back the last of his wine in one quick movement. "If you were at all acquainted with Eleanor, you would know *exactly* what I'm talking about!" he said meaningfully. "She has this way about her! She can make you say or do the very thing you wouldn't normally say or do under any other circumstance!"

"I must suppose, then," said Andrew, his face a mask of polite interest, "that you are entertaining second thoughts about the marriage?"

Charles looked at him in alarm and choked out a protest. "Here! I have said too much! I never should have spoken! Not to you—although you are a fine gentleman, to be sure! But it wouldn't do to discuss the matter with any other but Eleanor. Though God knows how I am to do it!" he ended, pitifully.

"Yes, I do see what you mean," said Andrew, with a sardonic curl to his lip. "A nasty business, to be sure, to have to tell the woman you were never really engaged to that you cannot marry her after all."

"Don't I know it, just!" said Charles, mistaking sarcasm for empathy. He helped himself to another glass of Madeira. "To be truthful, I was half-hoping she would have met someone here in London. All those balls and parties and such, and Eleanor a pleasant enough girl and rather decent-looking. If only she had caught the coattails of some London gentleman, I wouldn't be in this situation now!"

The sparks of light in the depths of Andrew's eyes

fanned to a new intensity. "How very inconsiderate of her, to be sure!"

This time, Charles caught the mordant note in Andrew's voice. "You mistake my meaning, sir!" he said, with a sharp look. "It is only since she has been in London that I have realized that—be we ever the best of friends—we shall never suit as man and wife! I was hoping she would come to the same realization, but instead her letters are filled with pledges of devotion and affection and the sort of gammon she has never pitched my way before, nor I hers! It's all very uncomfortable, I can tell you!"

"Were you never in love with Eleanor, then?" asked Andrew quietly, with a look of probing intensity.

Charles hesitated a moment, then slowly shook his head. "We've been tight and true since our cradle days. I taught her cricket and she taught me hedgerow shooting. If I ever considered her, it was more in a sisterly fashion than anything else! And then this business popped up of a London Season and Eleanor was beside herself. Worried herself into a frightful lather. Thought her father was going to force her to marry a noble nobody with an estate in the wilds of who-knows-where and she would never see her home again. That's when we decided to marry." Charles flashed a rather chagrined smile. "Our betrothal was more along the lines of a plot to keep her at Dessborough than an act of romantic devotion."

"I see," said Andrew, quietly. "Marrying Eleanor would have been nothing but a grand gesture on your part. Just the sort of thing one true friend would do for another."

"Exactly!" said Charles, pleased with Andrew's keen

grasp of the situation. "After all, we got on together right enough! There was no reason we shouldn't marry! But then she went off to London and left me quite alone. I had no one to turn to for companionship and a bit of heel kicking. Why, I should have been dulled to a doorknob had it not been for Georgianna—!" He stopped short, suddenly aware that he had verged on a gross indiscretion.

But Andrew considered that young Charles Adair had revealed more than enough already. He had long believed that Eleanor shared a grand passion with the young man to whom she was betrothed. Charles Adair, in one fell swoop, wrought a welcome injury to that notion.

He believed Charles when he said the engagement had been nothing but a pact between friends; just as he believed him when he said he and Eleanor had never shared an emotion any deeper than friendship.

A sudden sense of elation sprang to life within Andrew as he realized that Eleanor had been clinging to her betrothal to Charles Adair more from a sense of loyalty than affection.

He had a sudden thought and fixed Charles with a piercing look. "Is Eleanor acquainted with the young lady who has secured your affections?"

Charles flushed and sputtered for a moment before saying, "A gentleman would never reveal the name of a lady caught, through no fault of her own, in such a circumstance!"

"Eleanor shall ask about her, you know," said Andrew, quietly. He saw that Charles was regarding him with an expression mixed of confusion and horror, and said, "Eleanor shall want to know the identity of the young woman when you tell her you cannot go through with the betrothal. That is the reason you came here, is it not? To cry off?"

Charles Adair set his chin at a determined angle. "I—I have come here to confess the whole to Eleanor! I shall beg her forgiveness and understanding! Of course, if she will not hear me, I shall not draw back. No man of honor would jilt a lady! But I shall also be compelled to remind her that ours was never an acknowledged engagement. If we cry off now, no one shall ever know of the wretched business but Eleanor's father. Oh, and you, of course, Sir Andrew."

"You are very brave to tell her the truth," said Andrew.

Charles cast him a wretched look. "I should rather face the French Madman himself."

"Then perhaps I may be of assistance," said Andrew, his gaze never wavering from Charles Adair's expressive face.

Charles regarded him for an astonished moment. "*You*, sir?" he asked, incredulously. "Do you mean you would tell her for me?"

"Something of the like."

"Oh, I—I couldn't allow you, sir!" said Charles, clearly tempted by the offer.

"With the least effort, I believe you could."

Charles considered again for a moment, then squared his shoulders purposefully. "No! No, I am honor-bound to speak to Eleanor! What manner of coward should I be if I were to allow you to cast her off for me?"

"Ah, but I do not propose to jilt the lady on your behalf. Rather, I intend she should be brought to the realization that *she* must jilt *you*."

Clearly intrigued by the prospect, Mr. Adair said, "If you could manage such a thing, I should be eternally in your debt! Why, then I shouldn't have to confess to her my conduct and beg forgiveness and witness her tears and recriminations—" He broke off, as if suddenly coming to his senses, and said doubtfully, "But she never will. Cry off, that is. Eleanor is as loyal as a mastiff, with a much keener grip, once she sinks her teeth into a notion. She shall never let me go, if we leave it up to her."

"She will," said Andrew, confidently. "I've a notion that Eleanor wants to be released of her promise to you, as well, but she doesn't know it yet. Rely on me and do as I say, and you shall have a letter of release from Eleanor before the month is out."

These incredible words, spoken with such authority, easily overcame any possible objections Charles might have put forth. "I—I can't thank you enough! I know you are only doing this to spare Eleanor but—well, you have my gratitude, sir!"

"I also have you in the way should Eleanor choose this moment to return to the house. If you don't mind . . ." said Andrew, meaningfully, as his eyes strayed toward the door.

"Oh! Yes, of course! I shall take my leave straight away and leave for Dessborough first thing in the morning! You will get word to me, won't you, sir? You will let me know all is well with your plan?"

"You shall know all is well when you receive your letter of *congé* from Eleanor."

"I shall be on watch for it. By the end of the month, now—you promised!" reminded Charles with a dazzling smile of relief and happiness.

"Yes, yes! I shall promise anything if only you will leave *now,*" said Andrew.

Charles Adair cast him one last smile of gratitude before he left the room.

Once Charles was gone, Andrew poured out another glass of Madeira and took a negligent sip as he settled himself comfortably by the window, determined to await Lady Eleanor's return.

Chapter Sixteen

Eleanor had believed herself quite prepared to greet Andrew when next they met with calm, cool, good grace. She could not have been more mistaken.

From the moment the butler had informed her Sir Andrew de Ardescote awaited her pleasure in the blue drawing room, she had been battling back a flush of increasing intensity on her cheeks and a heart that insisted upon thumping wildly in her breast. By the time she laid a trembling hand upon the doorknob and prepared to enter the drawing room, she was rather amazed to find that her seriously weakened legs had been be able to carry her all the way up the stairs to the first floor.

She hesitated a moment, gathering her courage and considering the possible effect of throwing open the door and sweeping into the room in a grand manner. She quickly discarded such a notion, for her courage had been unreliably fragile since the night before when

Captain Lisle had escorted her from that small salon in Lady Seldon's home.

Eleanor instead slipped quietly into the room and silently shut the door. Andrew was standing at the tall windows, viewing the traffic on the street below; and she was able to watch him for a moment, unobserved. Curiously, she knew none of the emotions she had imagined she might feel upon seeing him again. No angry thoughts regarding his conduct or remembrances of betrayal rushed through her mind; instead, she could only stand there in silence, admiring the handsome figure he presented.

For a moment, she almost lost her resolve. For a moment her overwhelming love for him threatened to rout the promise she had made to herself that she would see him punished for his treatment of her; but in the end she was able to stand firm. She took a deep breath and silently renewed her pledge that she should see her plan succeed.

She took a few steps into the room and her movement caught his eye. He came to her immediately, clasping both her hands in his strong grip as his dark eyes searched her face with unnerving intensity.

His voice was low and, to Eleanor's ears, disarmingly gentle, as he said, "Eleanor! I had hoped you might receive me, but after my conduct the last time we met, I could not be sure."

Eleanor cast him a look of innocence. "Oh, Andrew, I don't believe your conduct last night to be any different than any other time!" She loosened her fingers from his grasp and moved away, half-afraid that his continued touch might divert her from her purpose.

Andrew's dark eyes followed her. He had not failed

to notice that she appeared a trifle withdrawn. He could detect the faint bruises of sleeplessness beneath her lovely blue eyes and he knew that he was the cause of her having lain awake all night.

But Eleanor spoke before he could put his concern into words. "Shall I see you this evening at Mrs. Beringer's masked ball?" she asked, striving for a light tone. "After all, it is due only to your efforts that my aunt, my cousin, and I were invited at all."

"Of course I shall be there, and I hope you shall do me the honor of saving a waltz in my name."

"By all means," she said. "To tell the truth, I am greatly looking forward to this evening. My aunt and I called upon Mrs. Beringer, you see, after she sent round our invitation. She was quite cordial to us and her home is quite magnificent. I was most impressed by the lovely terrace that runs along the length of the entire west side of the house."

Eleanor paused and smiled slightly in a manner calculated to convey a dreamy quality that effectively caught Andrew's attention. She said, in a rather breathless voice, "I thought the terrace rather magical and somehow romantic. I know you may think me foolish, but I had a dream about it, with the stars above gleaming through the darkness of the night. And in my dream, I stood on that terrace in the arms of a gentleman who—" She broke off abruptly, allowing Andrew to finish the remainder of the vision for himself.

He didn't disappoint her. Andrew crossed the distance between them in three long strides. Grasping her shoulders, he turned her to face him. In his eyes she saw again that mysterious light of passion smoldering in their dark depths.

He stood so close upon her that when she raised her face toward his, she found his lips were unnervingly near. It took every ounce of control she possessed to keep her thoughts to her task. Even then her hands trembled slightly against the hard wall of his muscled chest, and her voice was barely more than a whisper as she asked, "Andrew? Would you like to kiss me?"

At that moment he wanted nothing more in the world than to crush her in his arms and kiss her until she mewed like a helpless kitten. Instinctively, his arms tightened about her, forcing her head back against his shoulder in a manner that left exposed the smooth, white column of her slender neck.

"Oh, no! Not yet!" cried Eleanor, unable, within the circle of his arms, to divert her face, as she had planned. His strong embrace held her fast; and his breath warmly danced against her ear, stirring to life a curious fluttering deep within her. She hadn't anticipated that her body would respond in such a way to his simple touch, and it was all she could do to resist the temptation of seeing what other responses his nearness could evoke.

"Not here, Andrew," she said again. "On the terrace, tonight. Would you like to kiss me then?"

Andrew swallowed hard and mentally fought his way back through the hazy arousal that enveloped him. "Tonight?" he repeated, as if in a fog.

"Yes, Andrew! Tonight on the terrace at Beringer House," said Eleanor, doing her best to stay on course and ignore the breathlessness in her own voice. "Just think how romantic and thrilling it shall be! I shall await you on the terrace, in some secluded spot where you may come upon me quite alone and undetected. But you shall know it is me for I shall be wearing a pale blue domino and a blue mask with a single plume. And you? What color shall you be wearing so I may know you?''

He was having a difficult time following her conversation while she was still standing so temptingly within the circle of his arms. ''Color? The domino I shall wear is a claret, I believe.''

''Oh, Andrew, how romantic it shall be! I shall await you on the terrace in my blue domino and you shall come upon me like a masked bandit, and when you kiss me I shall be quite thrilled!''

Andrew felt sure that if she continued to tease him in this fashion, he would have no qualms about crushing her in his arms and ripping that pale blue domino from her slender, pliant body; but he couldn't very well give voice to such inclinations. Instead, he smiled slightly and reluctantly loosened his hold of her. ''My darling Eleanor, if that is what you want, I shall not fail you.''

She smiled brightly in return. Really, men were not quite as clever as they would have one believe, she thought, with a good deal of satisfaction.

Aloud, she said, ''I knew I might rely on you. Oh, how much I look forward to tonight! But now, Andrew, I'm afraid you must leave me. If I am to have my dearest wish fulfilled this evening, I must have my rest now.''

Andrew, however, was reluctant to leave; not because he would have preferred to have spent the remainder of his morning in Eleanor's presence, which, of course, he would. Rather, he was reluctant to leave because Eleanor's dazzling smile had evoked within him a sudden feeling of unease. He knew a smile of triumph when he saw one and Eleanor's smile fit quite neatly into that category. Of a certain, she was plotting something, and he was immediately on his guard.

It would have taken very little effort on his part to take her in his arms once more and kiss her until she fully confessed the whole of whatever little scheme she had planned; instead, he brought her fingers to his lips for a lingering farewell.

Eleanor's breath caught in her throat as his lips brushed her fingertips. "You—you won't forget? I shall be wearing a pale blue domino—"

"And a blue mask with a single plume," finished Andrew, helpfully. "I shan't forget. Until tonight, then."

He was gone before Eleanor had a chance to succumb to the temptation of calling him back. She ran to the window and waited until he emerged from the house, then watched as he gracefully swung his large form up onto his mount and set off. As she watched him ride down the street, she was struck by how impressive a figure he cut. Truly, Sir Andrew de Ardescote was the handsomest man in London; and she felt a rather unexpected surge of pride when she considered that of all the ladies of his acquaintance, he wanted her.

On the other hand, Eleanor doubted that he should want her for very much longer, especially if her plan was at all successful. She knew she ran the risk of losing whatever affection he held for her, but the temptation to see Andrew and Lord Montfort suffer as much embarrassment as their odious wager had brought her, held an appeal she found impossible to resist.

She called for the carriage to be brought back around to the front of the house. A short time later, seated comfortably with a small bandbox on her lap and a discreet housemaid on the opposite seat, Eleanor was traveling down Bond Street in search of Lord Montfort. Luck was on her side for she immediately spied him coming from his tailor's shop. She opened the carriage door and called to him.

Lord Montfort hesitated. The memory of Sir Andrew de Ardescote's threats were too fresh in his mind to be ignored out of hand; but when Eleanor smiled at him in a clearly inviting manner, and held out her small, gloved hand, he was quite unable to resist. He clasped her hand and drew her down onto the street beside him.

Eleanor suppressed the involuntary shudder his touch evoked and forced a bright smile. "Good day, Lord Montfort! Do forgive me for accosting you in this manner, but I wish to speak with you. May we walk a little way together?" She cradled the small bandbox she carried in one hand and tucked her other hand into the crook of his arm. She said, conspiratorially, "Such a horrid scene at Lady Seldon's musicale last time we met! I fear you have formed a rather unflattering opinion of me."

Lord Montfort eyed her warily. "As a matter of fact, I have, rather!"

"And little wonder, to be sure," commiserated Eleanor, with an effort. "I'm afraid you mistook my hesitancy that night. You see, Lord Montfort, I very much wish to have you kiss me."

Lord Montfort's eyes widened perceptively. "You do? By jove, I knew it! And why shouldn't you, after all?"

"Just so! But, my lord, I would have wished for a more romantic setting. Such a horrid little room we were in and I was quite unprepared! I'm afraid you caught me unawares and I performed very badly. Can you ever forgive me?" she asked, amazed at how easily the loathsome words sprang from her lips.

Lord Montfort appeared very much confused. "Forgive you? I—I should think so!"

Eleanor looked up at him through her lashes in what she hoped to be a provocative manner. "Shall we try again, my lord?"

His tongue eagerly flicked across his lips. "T-Try again?"

"Yes! Tonight, at Mrs. Beringer's masked ball! Oh, say you shall attend, or my enjoyment of the evening will be quite impaired!"

"Of course I shall be there. Her cards are always hard to come by! Very tonnish affair!"

"Oh, my lord, it is my dearest wish that you should kiss me tonight at Beringer House. Perhaps we may find a quiet, secluded spot where we may be truly alone."

Lord Montfort willingly gave the matter his consideration. "Here now! There is a rather large terrace with hedges and arbors and such! I daresay we may slip away from the ballroom and be quite private there!"

"Oh, Lord Montfort, how clever you are!" cooed Eleanor. "Tonight we shall meet on the terrace of Beringer House where we shall share our first kiss. How romantic it shall be! You must be first to go out on the terrace and you must find a bench a little way apart, so we may be quite private. And once you are seated, I shall come to you. You mustn't stand or speak, for that would break the spell! But if you remain silent and allow me to sit beside you, then at long last we shall share the kiss we have both wanted for so long!"

Lord Montfort swallowed hard. "By God, I shall do it!"

Eleanor favored him with a dazzling smile. She tugged on his arm and they stopped walking, and she held out the bandbox. "My lord, so I shall know you, will you wear this?"

He took the box from her and lifted the lid. Inside was a blue mask with a single plume nestled atop a pale blue domino. He eyed her doubtfully. "Of course, if you wish it. But the wretched thing shall not look well on me. I've already a cloak of red to wear."

"Oh, no, my lord! The domino you wear must be the blue! Oh, please, my lord, do not wear red," she begged, prettily. "The blue of a robin's egg is of all things my favorite color! Do say you will please me in this small, insignificant way!"

For a moment she thought he would refuse, but apparently the prospect of kissing her and thereby winning the wager was a temptation too strong for Lord Montfort to resist.

"Oh, very well," he said at last, and with little good grace.

Eleanor suppressed the smile of victory that tugged at the corners of her lips. She tucked her hand again into the crook of his arm and propelled him back toward her waiting carriage, all the while speaking in gushing tones. "Oh, Lord Montfort, I shall be quite beside myself until at last we are together on the terrace at Beringer House. You won't forget now? You must stay seated and say not a word! And I shall come to you in the moonlight. You shall know me by the domino of claret that I shall be wearing. Then, at long last, we shall share a kiss. Do believe me, my lord, when I tell you that tonight shall be an evening you shall not soon forget!"

Lord Montfort flushed with anticipation as he

brought her hand to his lips. "Until tonight then!" he said, and he handed her up into the carriage.

No sooner had Lord Montfort resumed his perambulation up Bond Street than he heard his name called. Turning, he found Sir Andrew reining a magnificent chestnut in beside him and saying again, in a voice of authority, "Montfort!"

The memory of Sir Andrew de Ardescote's threats came to his lordship in a rush and he said cautiously, "M-Me?"

"Of course, you! Thankfully, Providence refrained from playing a collosal trick on humanity and inflicted only one of your kind upon us. Who else should I mean?"

Lord Montfort judged this to be a rhetorical question and, in an uncommon show of wisdom, made no reply.

Andrew fixed him with a basilisk stare. "Why were you speaking to Lady Eleanor just now?"

A moment's reflection convinced his lordship that Andrew de Ardescote could not very well pummel the life out of him on a public street. The notion gave him the courage to answer, rather defensively, "She approached me! Asked me to walk with her—tucked her hand in my arm! I could hardly refuse!"

"Then you didn't consider the matter clearly. Tell me, what was your conversation?"

This question struck Lord Montfort as odd, leaving him with the sudden and distinct impression that he held an advantage over his rival. His lordship's conversation with Eleanor, although conducted on a public street, had been (now that he came to consider it) one of discreet secrecy, obviously engineered by Eleanor so that their words should not be overheard or cause comment. This revelation had a powerful effect on Lord Montfort and he gazed up at Andrew with an expression of increasing insolence.

"As it happens, we were speaking of the Beringer masked ball," he said, unable to resist the impulse to gloat just a little. "Very insistent she was that she should be able to know me from the other guests. If you must have it, we have arranged an assignation!"

He knew a brief moment of satisfaction as Andrew's dark brows came together in a thunderous frown. "Careful what you say, Montfort," he warned.

But his lordship could not be contained. He had what he believed to be a clear and distinct advantage over Andrew. "True, 'pon my honor! Tonight at the masked ball you shall know me as the victor in our little skirmish, for Lady Eleanor has made it her intention that I should kiss her this very evening! There!" he said, triumphantly, perceiving that Andrew was at a momentary loss for words. "That's knocked the wind out of your sails!"

Indeed, Sir Andrew de Ardescote, upon hearing these words, was startled into silence. What the devil could Eleanor be up to? he thought, while endeavoring to maintain a stoic expression. Inwardly alert, he said in a disarmingly disinterested tone, "And where precisely is this rendezvous to take place?"

"Oh, no! Were I to tell you that, you should think me quite the fool!"

"More so than I do already? I think you need have no fear along *that* vein," replied Andrew, smoothly. "So, you intend that tonight you shall at last see our wager come to an end, eh? Tonight you shall kiss Lady Eleanor and she shall willingly return that kiss. That was our wager, was it not?''

''I need no reminder from you on that score!'' retorted his lordship. ''I'm very well able to recollect the terms of the thing! Yes, she shall kiss me willingly, and the whole business shall be witnessed by Trowbridge, mark my words! As a matter of fact,'' he added, with a flash of what he perceived to be poetic justice, ''you may care to witness the deed yourself, and welcome!''

''I may just do that,'' said Andrew, ''if I can sort you from the other guests in attendance. I daresay, this assembly being a masquerade, I may have a difficult time singling you out.''

''Oh, you shall know me for I shall be wearing a mask and cloak of Eleanor's selection,'' Lord Montfort replied, rather triumphantly. ''I shall wear a domino of pale blue. After all, the blue of a robin's egg is the Lady Eleanor's favorite color!''

Andrew cocked a brow. ''Is it? I had no idea.''

This remark set the seal on Lord Montfort's belief that he was in possession of the proverbial upper hand. ''And I shall wear a mask that Eleanor herself gave me.''

''Will you, now? Tell me, is that what you carry in that bandbox? Show me!''

Lord Montfort, confident of his impending victory, saw no reason to refuse this simple request. He opened the bandbox to reveal a blue mask adorned with a single plume.

Only through sheer force of will did Andrew suppress the smile that quivered at the corner of his mouth. He might have wished that the woman he loved was not quite so devious in her methods of exacting revenge, but he would have been less than honest to have denied that he was suddenly intrigued by the general turn of events and more than a little curious as to how she might have gained knowledge of the bet in the first place.

Had Andrew prided himself on being a man of virtuous character, he would have seized that exact moment to have warned Montfort off. But he was far more interested in seeing if Eleanor had the pluck to carry out her scheme than he was interested in saving Lord Montfort from the ridiculous fate she had planned for him.

The thought occurred to him that Eleanor's scheme very much appeared to have included Andrew in its effects, but this realization left his withers unwrung. Instead, he was quite captivated by the notion that life with Eleanor would no doubt contain very few dull moments.

"And the Lady Eleanor? What color shall she be wearing," asked Andrew, his voice and countenance impassive. He knew the answer to his question, of course, but he graciously allowed Lord Montfort to mouth a reply.

"Why, a dark color to be sure. I believe she said she shall wear a cloak of claret."

Andrew was satisfied that he had heard enough. "Perhaps I shall accept your offer, Montfort," he said. "I admit I am interested in seeing if you will scratch or run aground when it at last comes time to call the bet. Until tonight, then!"

Andrew turned his mount and rode away before his lordship had a chance to reply. A plan of counterattack had begun to form in his mind, and he had every intention of acting upon it if for no other reason than to teach his absurd love that she had met her match when it came to a battle of wits.

Chapter Seventeen

Eleanor was convinced that a masked ball was really the most fascinating entertainment. Long before the last of the guests crossed Mrs. Beringer's doorstep, her hand had been claimed for every dance by some masked and therefore delightfully unknown partner.

To each of these gentlemen she was similarly anonymous. Glory Beringer, in keeping with the theme of anonymity pervading her rather lavish affair, had introduced Eleanor merely as the Rose Domino. Eleanor's blond hair was dressed high upon her head and powdered to conceal its true color; and her gown was covered by the pale rose domino that deftly mirrored the faint flush of excitement that mantled her cheeks beneath the white velvet mask she wore.

Indeed, only Iris and Lady Glower were aware of her identity; for everyone to whom Eleanor had spoken about the masquerade was fully expecting her to be gowned in a cloak of pale blue. Her appearance in rose, then, caused little comment, except from Lady Glower, who had been bitterly disappointed in Eleanor's news earlier that evening that she would not be able to wear the pale blue domino after all.

Eleanor had concocted for her aunt's benefit a story of pre-masquerade jitters and an unfortunately spilt cup of chocolate that had ruined the new blue domino Eleanor had planned to wear. As she had hoped, her aunt had quite lovingly insisted that Eleanor wear her old rose domino to the ball. Lady Glower had even produced from the depths of an old trunk a white mask that suited Eleanor very well.

Truly, Eleanor disliked having to resort to such dishonesty with her aunt. But then she chanced to think of the tremendous satisfaction she would derive if her plan succeeded, and she muffled those feelings of conscience.

Eleanor's fifth partner in as many sets led her onto the dance floor and made a bow as the music started up. Through the slits of his mask, she saw him looking at her appreciatively.

He clasped her hand and led her through the first steps of the dance. "Fair Rose Domino," he said, in a deep voice, "I swear you are the loveliest creature here tonight. Won't you tell me who you are?"

"Why, sir! To do so would hardly be in keeping with the spirit of the evening," said Eleanor, as the movement of the dance sent them apart.

"You are a cruel beauty," he said, when they met once more. "I was convinced that I knew everyone here tonight, despite the masks and gowns. Then I met you, and I must confess you baffle recognition!"

"Then I have accomplished my purpose," she

replied, with the full intention of guarding her identity. She dared not jeopardize the success of her scheme by being recognized. To her admirer she said, in a lighthearted tone, "Surely, sir, you have not guessed the identity of everyone here. The ballroom is much too crowded and all the guests are in disguise!"

"I have eyes for no other but you," said her partner effusively, spurred in part by an abundance of champagne and an assurance that his identity would remain forever concealed behind his green mask.

He wasn't the first of Eleanor's partners to have behaved so. Anonymity seemed to have lent everyone in the room an element of courage they might not have otherwise known. Eleanor's dance partners flirted shamelessly with her. From behind the safety of her velvet mask, she laughed and listened to their lavish compliments.

But however much she smiled and danced, Eleanor was not diverted from her purpose. Her gaze never strayed far from the entrance to the ballroom as she watched for the arrival of either a tall, masculine figure dressed in a domino the color of claret, or a shorter guest garbed in a pale blue domino and a blue mask with a single plume.

"Do you know everyone in attendance tonight?" she asked of her partner. "I thought that man in the white domino was Mr. Tilney. And I believe the man beside him in red to be Captain Lisle. Do you think so, too, sir?"

"I think only that I am happy to have found you, fair Rose Domino," he replied, gallantly.

Eleanor laughed. "You must tell me who you are, for

it would only be proper that I should know the name of the man who showers such compliments upon me."

"You shall know me soon enough, for we unmask at midnight."

"Do we indeed? I am rather hopeful that there shall be some masks discarded before that hour." An enigmatic smile touched the corner of her lips as the music came to an end and her partner escorted her off the dance floor.

It was then that she spied the figure in blue on the far side of the room. She held no doubt that it was Lord Montfort, obediently garbed in the pale blue domino and plumed mask she had given him that very day. He was slowly making his way about the perimeter of the ballroom, and Eleanor guessed his objective was the multipaned glass doors that gave off onto the terrace.

A pang of conscience shot through her as she realized that in very little time she would cause her two most ardent suitors a significant degree of humiliation. It wasn't in her nature to make sport of another person. While she was able to convince herself that she cared not a jot that Lord Montfort should be held up to ridicule, she could not say she felt the same where Andrew was concerned.

Suddenly gone was her keen desire to see Andrew suffer for his horrid treatment of her. Instead, she knew an overwhelming determination to somehow foil the vengeful plot she herself had set in motion.

Instinctively, Eleanor began to make her way toward Lord Montfort, fully intending to tell him that he must not go out onto the terrace. Yet no sooner had she taken a single step, than she was intercepted by her next dance partner.

She was at a loss to know what to do until she hit upon the happy notion to send this gentleman off to procure for her a glass of lemonade. Her request was not, in fact, a mere ruse to be rid of her partner, for her throat had gone uncomfortably dry as she spied Lord Montfort disappearing through the glass doors.

With her partner dispatched in one direction, Eleanor set off in the other and quickly followed Lord Montfort out onto the terrace.

The soft glow of candlelight from the ballroom shone through the windows and upon the terrace, and the stars glowed brightly in the sky above. With its decorative stone balustrade and ornamental arbors and hedges casting shadows upon its marbled surface, the terrace was just as romantic a setting as Eleanor had thought it would be. But her thoughts were far from those of a romantic turn. Her only purpose now was to prevent Andrew and Montfort from meeting.

She looked about quickly and spied Lord Montfort on the far end of the terrace just as he disappeared into the shadows of an arbor set amidst the rows of a yew hedge. As she stood, undecided what she should do next, she saw another figure, cloaked and masked in the color of claret, emerge from the ballroom.

The odd sensation of moving through a nightmare came over Eleanor. Her mind refused to function and her feet remained firmly planted, unwilling to move, as she watched the figure in claret follow Lord Montfort into the shadows.

The enormity of her actions dawned upon her. She tried to call Andrew's name, but her voice, when it at last came to her, was barely above a whisper.

She tried again to call after him, and this time she

was a bit more successful. The sound of her own voice saying his name provided the impetus that at last spurred her to action. "Andrew, please wait!" she cried, but barely had she taken a step when another figure sprang from seemingly nowhere to block her path.

Eleanor collided with the figure with a thud and a gasp. It took a moment for her to realize that a man—and a rather large one, at that—cloaked and masked in black, prevented her progress.

Instinctively, Eleanor retreated several steps, but the stone balustrade against her back prevented her from moving far. The figure in black advanced relentlessly upon her.

"Let me pass!" demanded Eleanor, her thoughts still turned to the task of warning Andrew off his purpose. "Please, I must get by!"

But the shadowy figure before her made it impossible for her to do just that. On either side of her he planted a hand on the balustrade.

Eleanor looked up into his face with wide, uncertain eyes; but his black mask revealed nothing but the glitter of dark eyes in the moonlight.

"Oh, please let me by! I have made a horrid, odious mistake and I must stop Andrew!" she cried, pushing ineffectually against the unknown's chest.

To her astonishment, he ignored her pleas and, wrapping an arm around her waist, he pulled her up against him. With his free hand he reached behind her to loosen the strings of her mask.

"Stop! Stop this instant!" cried Eleanor, with more alarm than fright, but the strings were untied and the mask fell away before she could make any further protest. In the next instant, his lips were on hers.

Eleanor struggled against him, but his hold on her was a stronger one than she had ever known. She pushed strenuously against the wall of his chest and he, in response, tightened his arms about her slim waist and shoulders.

The movement of his hands across her back sent a wave of feeling through her. Only one man had ever before evoked such a response. In a rush did she recall that her senses had reacted in very much the same way whenever Andrew took her in his arms to dance with her; and that very morning he had held her in a manner that had left her trembling and breathless, much as she now was in the arms of the masked unknown.

The revelation came to her just as he released her lips; but still Eleanor could not quite trust her instinct. She raised a tentative hand to his shadowed face and lightly traced the firm, square outline of his jaw. "Andrew?" she breathed in a wondrous tone. "Andrew, it *is* you!"

He smiled then, a brilliant, victorious smile that caught the moonlight in a dazzling display. He lowered his head toward hers once again, but she planted her fingertips firmly upon his lips, saying, through a bewildered yet happy fog, "I—I don't understand! Andrew, if *you* are kissing *me,* then who, pray, is kissing Lord Montfort?"

Much as he would have relished doing so, Andrew was given no opportunity to answer; for at that moment the darkness of the evening was pierced by the yelp of two distinctly outraged male voices.

"Rest assured, my diabolical darling," he said, with great satisfaction, "that at least one of those atrociously feral voices came from Montfort. The other, I do believe, belongs to Trowbridge."

Eleanor's head was swimming slightly. "Lord Trowbridge? But, why should he kiss Lord Montfort when all the time I thought—" Her words halted abruptly as she realized she had verged on an ill-timed confession of sorts.

Andrew smiled slightly, leaving Eleanor with little doubt that he had never for a moment been fooled by her horrid plan for revenge.

"I know what you thought, and I'm quite impressed that you very nearly carried it off. But Montfort is a man of limited discretion, and Trowbridge, a man of less-than-keen understanding. Between the two of them, I was able to orchestrate a counterplot to the one you concocted."

Eleanor shook her head slightly, as if to clear it. "But what, pray, has Lord Trowbridge to say to the purpose?"

"He merely became an unwitting accomplice," said Andrew, gently. "I recruited Geoffrey Lisle to visit Montfort and claim poverty. He was most convincing, apparently, for by the time he took his leave, he had convinced Montfort that he hadn't the blunt to purchase a domino to wear tonight. Montfort quite obligingly lent him the red one he had planned to wear—until, of course, you enticed him to wear the blue." He glanced speculatively down at her upturned face, poised so temptingly close to his own. "Someday you must show me what wiles you used to convince Montfort to do your bidding. In fact, I think I shall insist upon a most thorough demonstration." He tightened his arms about her and heard her breath catch most becomingly between her parted lips.

"It—it was not as you think," she said in a seriously weakened voice.

"No? Indulge me. Use that astonishingly fertile imagination of yours to make something up."

Eleanor trembled slightly as his hand moved again across her back. She held little doubt that he knew the effect his touch had upon her and that he reveled in that knowledge. She looked up into his face, searching for some sign that he, too, felt the same stunning warmth that she felt rippling through her own body; but the shadowed mask he wore yielded no clue to his feelings. Every touch of his hands on her body, every hint of his breath upon her brow sent a wave of reaction through her that resulted in an ever-deepening sense of befuddlement. She could only hope that he didn't choose that moment to release her, for her mind was so muddled and her body so overwhelmed by the intimacy of his powerful form pressed against hers, that she seriously doubted that her legs would be able to support her.

She struggled to maintain some level of coherent thought as Andrew's lips danced seductively against the delicate skin just below her ear. "But—but you haven't finished telling me about Lord Trowbridge."

Andrew smiled slightly. In his time he had held his fair share of women in his arms, but none that he recalled had ever responded to his embrace quite as delightfully as Eleanor. He was half tempted to see if he couldn't once again make her breath catch in that tantalizingly wanton manner he had observed a mere moment before. In fact, he was sure it would take very little effort on his part to prove to her just how futile her efforts to maintain a sense of normalcy really were.

But some niggling sense of better judgement routed him. He couldn't, after all, pursue his desire for her on a darkened terrace where the threat of discovery by other guests loomed larger than he had hitherto realized. The satisfaction of at last holding Eleanor in his arms had superseded his better judgement—until now.

He took a deep, steadying breath and silently vowed that the next time he held her, he wouldn't allow her to get away so easily. Then he loosened his hold slightly, enough so that his newfound resolve to behave himself where she was concerned should not be shaken.

"Ah, Trowbridge, to be sure," he murmured, forcing himself to concentrate. "I recruited Lisle for yet another tour of duty. He had proved himself so adept at duplicity that I next dispatched him to visit Trowbridge, who was very easily convinced that his good friend Montfort stood in jeopardy of losing that beastly wager because he was deep in his cups and couldn't make sufficient sense of himself to attend the ball tonight. After that, it was very easy for Lisle to persuade Trowbridge that if he were indeed a true friend, he would contrive to somehow cover Montfort's bet. The fact that Lisle just happened to have in his possession the domino of claret that I was supposed to wear provided the final inducement. Trowbridge took my domino, thinking it to be Montfort's, and came here tonight with the full intention of kissing you in Montfort's stead, thereby claiming victory for his friend."

Eleanor looked up at him appreciatively. "A truly monstrous plot! And what, pray, do you think shall happen next?"

"Judging from the commotion coming from the other side of that arbor, I don't believe either Montfort or Trowbridge will ever speak of the wager or you again. Should either be foolish enough to do so, they shall risk public ridicule from which they may never recover." Andrew smiled down upon her. "I believe we shall hear no more talk of warming Lady Chill with a kiss," he said, visibly pleased with the manner in which the whole affair had ended.

But Eleanor was far from pleased. His words had produced the same effect as a pail of cold water being doused upon her head. That she had full knowledge of the bet and of Andrew's involvement with it, was one thing; but to have him stand before her and speak of that beastly wager with no apparent concern for the humiliation and suffering he had caused was another thing altogether.

In one sudden and overwhelming rush, all the feelings of betrayal and disgrace came back to her. She felt herself stiffen within the yielding circle of his arms and she said, her voice quiet with disapproval, "You seem very well satisfied with the way the entire affair has turned out."

"I am, rather," he said. A hint of a boyish smile touched the corners of his lips.

Eleanor turned her head away as he pulled her against him once more. She hated to ask the question, but some perverse impulse told her she had to know. "How much did you win?"

"Win?" he repeated, as he nuzzled his chin against the sweet softness of her curls. "What do you mean?"

"I am talking of the wager. How much did you win from Lord Montfort?"

Andrew looked down at her with a slightly confounded expression. "Now what, I wonder, would prompt you to ask such a thing?"

"You did win the bet, didn't you?" pursued Eleanor, rather relentlessly. "You did kiss me before Lord Montfort did. And it seems to me that you went to quite a bit of trouble indeed to do so."

A stricken look crossed Andrew's face as the meaning of her words dawned upon him. "On the contrary, I released myself from that bet tonight by taking Montfort out of the running."

"And collected for yourself a rather sizeable sum besides, I should think."

He was still wearing his mask, but Eleanor was quite convinced that behind it one dark brow was flying ominously.

He drew himself up to his full and towering height, but his voice was quiet as he said, "My actions here tonight were not designed to win that blasted wager. Good God, Eleanor, tonight I saved your reputation!"

"You mean the reputation that you alone were responsible for sullying in the first place?"

Her words, spoken with as much disciplined dignity as she could muster, threw him quite off his stride. He released her and moved away slightly, as if he needed time and space in which to think. He reached up and untied the laces of his mask and, as it fell away, he turned to face her. He was frowning, and for the first time since she had made his acquaintance, he appeared to be unsure himself.

"Eleanor, I was deep in my cups that night," he said, slowly and deliberately, alert to her slightest reaction. "Had I not been so, I assure you, I never would have embarked upon such loathsome behavior as to make you or any other woman the object of a boorish wager.''

"Were you in your cups when you met me at Hookham's library?'' she asked, and knew the dubious satisfaction of seeing him blanch visibly. "Or when you danced with me at Almack's? Or drove me to the Gardens? Were you in your cups then, too?''

"You know I was not,'' he said grimly, his eyes never leaving her face.

"So you might have called off the whole abominable business. You might have, but you didn't. For to do so would mean that you could not possibly win the wager.''

He shook his head slightly, as if somehow she had got all her facts wrong. "Eleanor, my name was at stake!''

"And to save it, you were willing to soil mine.''

Of a sudden, Sir Andrew de Ardescote, the most polished Corinthian in England, was burningly aware of his own clumsiness. He lost no time in making matters worse. "Eleanor, I regret my actions—all of them. Why, I should never have kissed you—I know that now!''

Eleanor stared at him, hardly able to credit that she had heard him correctly. "You—you regret *kissing* me? I suppose were it not for that beastly bet, you never would have brought yourself to kiss me at all!''

"Of course I wouldn't have kissed you without the bet,'' he retorted, unable to understand her sudden flash of anger or the depths to which his own awkward explanations were taking him. "Eleanor, you must realize that were it not for the wager, I shouldn't have taken you up in the first place!''

Even in the shadows of the darkened terrace, he saw her cheeks flame and knew he had misspoken yet again. He hadn't felt so awkward and inept in front of a woman since his days as a youth, and the feeling did not sit well. He made a move toward her, but halted when he detected the nearby presence of another pair of masked guests strolling close upon them.

An uneasy silence stretched between them as they waited for the strangers to pass by. Eleanor used those few uncomfortable moments to steel herself against whatever other horrid revelations Andrew might choose to reveal before the evening was over.

Bravely, she fought against the threat of tears that pricked the backs of her eyes. Beastly man! Not content with humiliating her in public, he had the insulting nerve to suggest that he might never have paid the least attention to her were it not for that abominable bet. She half expected him to declare that all the time she was warming to him and well on her way to falling in love with him, he had no clearer purpose than to collect his winnings and move along to the next sporting event.

Now, when any but a monster of insensitivity should have seen how stunned and hurt she was by such revelations, and how few words it would take to set everything back to rights and give her some more encouraging picture of his feelings for her, he chose to remain silent.

She chanced a look at him and saw that he was drawn to his full and commanding height and his stance was stiff. He returned her look with an unnerving frown, his dark eyes never wavering. Hardly the gaze of a man looking upon the face of his beloved, she realized, with a renewed effort to control her threatening tears.

She clasped her hands together in a grip that provided a measure of self-control. "I notice you still do not deny your winnings," she said, with a shaking voice and a fervent prayer that he would at last say something—

*any*thing—that would reveal a scant tenderness of feeling for her.

But the words that were forming in Andrew's mind were far from the loverlike bromides of Eleanor's imagining. In fact, he was of a good mind to clasp her shoulders, give her a hearty shake, and ask what the devil she meant by thinking such ill of him. The timely passing of yet another masked and gowned couple perambulating about the romantically moonlit terrace prevented Andrew from acting on his inclination. He was able, however, to discharge a certain amount of the annoyance he felt by directing a wrathful stare upon the encroaching couple that very effectively quickened their steps and sent them speedily on their way.

He turned back toward Eleanor with the full intention of explaining, in as many words as necessary, that he didn't care a whit for the wager, the winnings, or anything else but Eleanor's regard.

That was his intention; but he was given no opportunity to act upon it, for turning back toward the balustrade against which Eleanor had been standing, he realized she was gone.

Chapter Eighteen

Iris observed Eleanor's threateningly quivering lower lip and felt perilously close to tears herself. "Oh, Mama, please don't plague her any longer! You must see how distressed poor Eleanor is!" She went to her cousin, who was seated rigidly on the edge of a very elegant settee. Iris sat beside her, draped a comforting arm about her shoulders, and said kindly, "Dearest cousin, I am in complete sympathy with you and understand your decision, of course!"

"Well, *I* don't understand it," interjected Lady Glower, in a somewhat frustrated fashion. "I cannot fathom that you should be so anxious to abandon a successful Season and return to Dessborough Place. Child, you have attended only the best parties and assemblies; the patronesses of Almack's were quite delighted with you; and you had Sir Andrew de Ardescote—of all people!—in your pocket for the better part of a month. And now, when your stay in London has proved to be much more triumphant than I had ever *dared* hope, *you* want to *leave!*"

Eleanor clasped her hands together in her lap and said in a voice of quiet control, "Dear Aunt, I know you are disappointed in me, but please believe me when I tell you I must return home. My Season was, as you say, quite wonderful; and I thank you for it. But my stay in London is over and it is time for me to go home where I belong."

Lady Glower was on the verge of informing her tiresome niece that she wouldn't have it—that she wouldn't tolerate such hoydenish behavior—that it was wrong for Eleanor to have sent off a note to her father that he should expect her immediate return and to have ordered her trunks packed and readied for travel. But in the two days since she had attended Glory Beringer's masquerade, Eleanor had quite competently done just so.

In Lady Glower's opinion, Eleanor was obviously headstrong, but she had always been a rather sensible girl who could be made to see the unreasonableness of her actions. In this instance, however, Lady Glower's remonstrances had borne no effect upon her.

She considered the notion of trying again, of demanding that Eleanor tell her the reason behind her singular notion that she must leave London—and in such an uncommonly precipitous fashion—but one look at Eleanor, bravely fighting back the veil of tears that clouded her blue eyes, and Lady Glower's heart melted.

She said in a far softer tone than she had yet used that morning, "I cannot help but think you are making the gravest of mistakes, my dear."

Eleanor nodded slightly, acknowledging her aunt's words, but she didn't trust herself to offer any further reply, lest she lose the careful control she had managed to maintain over the last two days.

The sound of a commotion from the street below sent Lady Glower to the window. "I see the chaise has been brought around. Your trunks will be put aboard shortly, and I shall have a word with Mary about her duties during your journey. You must promise to send Mary back to me directly, for I'm sure I don't know how I am to go on without her."

"Thank you for allowing me your abigail," said Eleanor dutifully. "I shall send her back straight away as soon as I have arrived home."

Lady Glower drew her attention from the scene outside the window and observed her niece with a keen concern. "There is still time to change your mind," she said, holding out every hope that her niece would do just so. "You might stay just long enough for me to send for your father. You know you may depend upon him to come for you, especially once he has been told how unhappy you are. My dear, I'm quite aware that you do not wish to speak to me of the source of your unhappiness—I daresay you haven't even confided to Iris what has occurred. But I cannot help but think you shall only be making matters worse by this rash course you have chosen to embark upon!"

Once again, Eleanor felt the tears prick the backs of her eyes and she clasped her hands ever tighter in her lap. "I—I just want to go home," she said, in such a piteously small voice that Lady Glower felt herself truly alarmed.

That such an intrepid, spirited girl as Eleanor had

always proven herself to be should be reduced to such a sorry state of misery as she now appeared convinced Lady Glower as nothing else could that her niece should have her way. "Very well, I shall say nothing more," she promised, crossing the room to clasp Eleanor's hands and draw her to her feet. "Dearest child, my one wish is that you should be happy. Gracious, that is the only reason you came to me in the first place—to see you happy and to give you a most dazzling Season. That, I do believe, we have accomplished most splendidly, and I think it brought you some happiness. Now you tell me that only a return home shall make you happy? Then I shall not twit you over it any further. I may not agree with the scheme, but I shan't forbid you to go! There! I shall take my farewell of you now while we are quite alone and without the prying eyes of servants who are sure to be lingering about in the hall. Be a good girl and give your aunt a kiss."

To hear her aunt speak so tenderly almost provided Eleanor with the final inducement to burst into tears. But once again she was able to hold her overwrought emotions in check and dutifully bestowed upon her aunt's cheek an affectionate salute.

"Dear Aunt, thank you for letting me come to you."

"And I expect you shall come to me once again, in due course," said Lady Glower, feeling somewhat misty-eyed herself. "Now, I must go to Mary and see that she is properly mindful of her duties in caring for my dear niece." She enveloped Eleanor in a brief but fond embrace and left the room, saying, "I shall see you presently in the hall."

As the door closed upon Lady Glower, Eleanor breathed a small sigh of relief, believing that the most troubling portion of the ordeal she had been made to bear was at last coming to an end. She turned toward Iris, saying in a falsely bright voice, "Thank goodness that's over! I do love your mama, Iris, but making one's farewells with a doting aunt can be quite tiresome, I assure you!"

Iris smiled slightly. "Shall you think me tiresome, too, if I tell you that I shall miss you dreadfully? And will you be bored to know that I am in complete agreement with Mama that your notion to leave London might turn out to be a most dreadful mistake." She watched Eleanor's small hands begin to work together in agitation and asked, quietly, "Have you said goodbye to Sir Andrew?"

Eleanor strove for a presence of outward calm, even as she felt a warm flush mantle her cheeks. "Oh, I took my leave of Sir Andrew two nights ago at Mrs. Beringer's masquerade. I doubt he shall have any desire to further our friendship, for it has quite served its purpose. He got what he wanted from the acquaintance, and I certainly have what I wanted—I am going home, after all!"

Iris observed this show of bravado with a small frown of concern. "Dearest Cousin, won't you see him? Won't you at least send him a note, however brief, telling him of your intentions?"

"And why, pray, should I do that?" Eleanor went to a side chair on which she had deposited the bonnet and gloves she intended to wear on her journey and made a great show of smoothing imaginary creases from the pristine garments. "He knows as well as I that it was ever my intention to return home at the first opportunity."

"But—but his *feelings* for you—"

"Are quite nonexistent," asserted Eleanor.

"I shall never believe that," said Iris firmly.

Eleanor's slim shoulders shrugged disinterestedly. "Believe what you like, but the fact remains that I am leaving London this morning!"

"Without saying goodbye?" came a deep, masculine voice from the door that so startled Eleanor, she almost jumped out of her shoes.

She recognized Andrew's voice immediately, of course, although she dared not look at him. She knew only that those three simple words he had uttered had borne a most dramatic effect upon her senses.

Her hands, which a mere moment before had been so elegantly splayed across the fine kid fabric of her gloves, had begun to tremble violently. And her mind, once so determined and resolute, was transformed in an instant to a muddied jelly of confusion.

Apparently, Andrew's arrival had no such effect upon Iris. She went to him, with her hand outstretched and the dreamy quality of a true romantic in her expression. "Sir Andrew! How splendid! I—I *knew* you wouldn't fail!"

"Did you?" he asked, bending most properly over her fingertips while his gaze never wavered from Eleanor's face. "Then you are more well acquainted with my character than I am myself. I had thought of calling to see if you might receive me, Eleanor. I never supposed to find you intent upon throwing dust in my eyes."

She spun around to face him, her chin set at a martial angle. "Throw dust in your eyes? No such thing, I assure you! Why, the traveling chaise is at the front door, very much in view of the whole of London! And you make it sound as if I were sneaking off like a Turkish tent-maker!''

"She's leaving," said Iris, giving Andrew's fingers a meaningful squeeze before she allowed him to withdraw his hand. "She's going back to Dessborough Place as soon as her trunks have been packed aboard the chaise.''

"Is she? Then I have arrived just in time to make my farewells. Shall I do so now, Eleanor?''

Eleanor ventured a quick look at him, but his expression was unreadable. He had spoken so calmly, as if saying goodbye to her would require no more emotion than flicking a speck of lint from his immaculate cuff. Cold, unfeeling beast! It would never do for her to show just how much his presence disturbed her. If he insisted upon behaving with such chivalrous conceit, she would, she determined, match him courtesy for courtesy.

Her chin rose a notch and she said in regal accents, "I shouldn't dream of leaving London without first saying goodbye to you!''

"Then I hope you shall do so properly," he said, opening the door and training an expectant eye upon Iris. "Miss Glower, would you be so kind?''

Eleanor's hard-won composure deserted her. "No! Iris, you mustn't leave! That is—I—I haven't yet bid my cousin a proper goodbye and—oh, Iris, do stay!''

Iris chose that moment to reveal a rather traitorous side to her character. She clasped Eleanor in a smothering embrace, saying, "I wish you happy, dear, dear Cousin! Please listen to whatever Sir Andrew has to say and—and I shall see you in the hall presently!''

Eleanor meant to respond quite intelligently, but she was so distracted by her cousin's defection and the pros-

pect of being left alone with Andrew that the words of
farewell that tumbled from her mouth were little more
than an incoherent jumble. She saw that her efforts had
sent one of Andrew's dark brows soaring with appreciation as he courteously closed the door behind Iris.

His whole manner was quite past bearing; while she
was fighting to stay afloat of her turbulent emotions,
he was gazing at her with calm, good grace. It was most
unchivalrous of him to look so composed.

And so handsome. He had entered the room with his
gloves and hat still in his hand, as if he had arrived at the
house and mounted the stairs to the first-floor drawing
room in too great a hurry to have disposed of them
properly. Now he removed his cloak, a heavy,
multicaped garment that swung gracefully from his tall
frame, and he deposited these items on a nearby chair
with disarming negligence. He was in driving dress, his
broad shoulders molded into an elegantly tailored coat
that somehow managed to accentuate, rather than hide,
his strength.

Blushing slightly, Eleanor recalled the feeling of his
powerful arms about her and the exhilarating sensations
his touch had stirred within her. Andrew, she perceived,
was laboring under no such recollection.

He had the appearance of one who was about to
pass a most affable morning, and to prove it, he said,
cordially, "So, you are off to—Dessborough, is it?"

Eleanor's chin came up. "That's right. It is my home,
as you'll recall. As soon as my trunks and cases are
aboard the chaise, I shall be leaving."

"Ah, then that won't be for some time. You see, the
men were working so hard, and looking so abominably

hot, I sent them round to the kitchens for a cooling drink."

"You—you *didn't!*" Eleanor said in disbelief, going immediately to the window. Below, the walkway was deserted but for a lone sentinel groom sitting atop an abandoned pile of trunks and bandboxes.

She turned to confront Andrew and saw that his mouth was cocked in an odd little smile.

"Don't eat me," he said. "They shall return to their labors presently. In the meanwhile, you and I might pass the time together. I hate hasty goodbyes, don't you?"

Not as much as she hated the complacent expression on his face. The urgent need to punish him for his behavior seized her. "You cannot know how relieved I am to hear you say so!" she exclaimed with a flair that would have put Sarah Siddons to the blush. "I quite thought you would cut me. After all, I did use you shamefully and I could hardly blame you at all if you never spoke to me again!"

Andrew eyed her keenly, wondering from what non-sensical notion her words sprang. "Not speak to you? Why shouldn't I?"

"Surely you know that from the day I made your acquaintance, my behavior has been nothing short of mercenary," she said, brightly. "And I did merely use our friendship to further my ambition to leave London. You'll recall that was my plan all along—to return home and marry Charles Adair."

Andrew's dark brows came together. "Is that still your intention, Eleanor?"

"Of course!" she insisted with a slight laugh that was more hollow than carefree. "We embarked upon a bargain, of sorts, you and I. You won your wager and I gained an early return home. I only hope you will forgive the fact that my treatment of you was horribly self-serving and shabby!''

There, it was out. She had yet again brought up the subject of that monstrous bet in the hopes that he would at last admit that he was wrong to have ever engaged in such a wager, that he would admit his horrid treatment of her and apologize for it. But no such words came from his lips. Instead, he merely stood regarding her with an unreadable expression.

He picked up his cloak, and for a brief moment, Eleanor was half-afraid he might once again drape it about his shoulders and take his French leave of her. But instead, he drove his long fingers within the folds of the garment and withdrew from its volume a harlequin's mask.

Eleanor recognized it as soon as she saw it; the pale blue mask with the single plume was the very one she was supposed to have worn to the masquerade ball, but had instead given Lord Montfort.

''I found this on the terrace after you left the other night. You know, I don't believe I ever had a chance to see you in it,'' said Andrew in a quiet voice as he began a slow, deliberate advance upon her. ''You told me you would be wearing this mask when you so tantalizingly persuaded me to meet you on the terrace. I should still like to see you in it. Say you will put it on. If only for a moment.''

So this is how it felt to be beguiled, thought Eleanor, defenseless against his overwhelming nearness and the seductive tone in his voice. She could barely breathe, to say nothing of moving, as he gently brought the mask up in front of her face.

She felt his other hand at the back of her head, tentatively at first; then his long fingers plunged amid her curls to possessively draw her to him.

"Just as I suspected," he said, his voice coming deeply. "With this mask in place, all but your most bewitching charms are hidden and I see only the beauty of your eyes and the soft fullness of your lips."

Somehow, without even thinking, Eleanor had moved closer and found herself within the circle of his arms. Her reaction to his embrace was just as wonderful as it had been that evening on the terrace of Beringer House. He took the mask away so it was no longer between then, and his lips were perilously close to hers.

How easy it would be to let him kiss her! She wanted the kiss so very much and she could tell by the shadow of passion that lurked within the glittering depths of his eyes, that he felt very much the same way.

But she knew just as surely that a kiss was not enough. He had, after all, kissed her before merely to win that wretched wager.

Or had he? There was only one way she would ever know if he had kissed her that night out of avarice or attraction. She had to hear the right words from Andrew, for they alone could salve the wounds his unfeeling wager had dealt her heart. She waited, breathlessly, willing him to say the simple phrases that would tell her all she needed to know. Yet no such sentiments escaped the finely chiseled lips poised so close above hers.

It took every ounce of self-will she possessed to steel herself against the manner in which her heart was pounding and her breath was coming in short fluttering bursts—but she did it. She pushed against the hard wall of his broad chest, and he released her.

Leaving the heady circle of his arms was the hardest thing she had ever done, but she managed it somehow and put a sufficient distance between them to ensure she wouldn't be so likely to succumb to further temptation.

"I'm sure my trunks will have been stowed by now," Eleanor said in a wooden little voice. She picked up her bonnet and set it with deliberate care upon her head, deeply aware of Andrew's eyes upon her. She ventured to look up into his face, and saw that his frown had deepened and his dark eyes were gleaming.

"Do you mean to tell me you still intend to leave? Now? Knowing how I—"

Eleanor's head came up and she asked breathlessly, "Knowing how you what?"

He glared at her. "So you intend to return home after all! No doubt to marry Charles Adair!" He took a step towards her, and demanded, savagely, "Tell me that you are in love with Adair! Look me in the eye and tell me so!"

She couldn't. She had long since realized that any affection she felt for Charles was on a scale of a life-long friend, and she could not consider professing a passion for him knowing full well that it was Andrew she loved. But she could hardly be the one to make such an admission first, and Andrew, staring down at her with a thunderous expression, didn't appear to be a man about to voice his most tender feelings.

She had never heard him speak so roughly before. He certainly had ill chosen the time to reveal that side of his character. Eleanor had looked to him for comfort and he had responded with anger; she had sought from him some sign of affection and he had instead offered furious resentment.

She found it a little difficult to think clearly and turned her attention to the ribands on her bonnet; but her hands were trembling and her mind was in such a muddled whirl that despite her attempts, she could achieve no better than a rather lamentable and ridiculously lopsided bow.

She was still blindly struggling with the ribands when she realized with a start that he had crossed the distance between them and was standing quite close upon her. He covered her small hands with his own, stilling her efforts; then he set his nimble fingers to the task and arranged the ribands quite respectably. His warm fingers lingered under her chin and he gently nudged her head back so he could look down into her eyes. "Don't go."

A prudent woman would have accepted that with those two simple words Sir Andrew de Ardescote, the Fashionable Corinthian, had made an admission of monumental significance.

But Eleanor was feeling far from prudent. Rather, she was more convinced than ever, as she looked up into his handsome face, that she was quite hopelessly in love with him. She was equally determined that she should not be left alone in love.

She looked up at him, silently pleading that the next words from his mouth would be the ones she was longing to hear. She waited, but the words didn't come. Andrew merely stood regarding her with a frowning gaze of unnerving intensity.

Eleanor turned away and scooped up her gloves to

draw them on with still-quaking fingers. "If only you knew to what lengths I have gone to orchestrate this journey—and on such short notice!—you would not be so quick to ask me to abandon it now. I—I simply *cannot* change my plans without being given *some* reason to do so," she said, unable to resist the impulse to provide him with one more opportunity to redeem himself.

"What game is this?" Andrew demanded, frowning again. "Eleanor, if you hate me for what I've done, say so!"

She looked at him hopefully. "And if *you* are truly sorry for what you've done, will *you* not say so?"

For a moment he was too confounded to speak. "Eleanor, I explained what occured when I embarked upon that wager. My reputation was at stake! My consequence—"

"Has been heartily drummed into my ears since the day I arrived in London," enjoined Eleanor, at last abandoning all hope of ever hearing the loverlike confession of her dreams. "You reminded me of your worth yourself the first time we drove out together, do you remember? You asked me if your consequence meant nothing to me and, to own the truth, it does not. For *you* hold it in enough regard for both of us!"

Thunderstruck, he retorted, "You make me sound like some kind of arrogant liege lord!"

"No, not that. But I don't think you have ever in your life done anything without first determining how it shall affect your consequence. Have you never acted incautiously, without considering what people shall think? Have you never found yourself so overwhelmed by the mere sensibility of the moment, that you never gave a thought to your reputation? Why, even now you are quite willing to—'' She stopped short, realizing that she was about to reveal how much he had hurt her.

If ever there was a time for Andrew to say something of his feelings, this was it. She cast him one last look of encouragement and saw that he was staring at her, his eyes narrowed and dark brows frowning, and his mouth pursed into a grim line of resolve. Not the expression of a man about to confess, at long last, his feelings for her.

There was nothing for it but to escape his presence before she lost the mastery of the tears that once again pricked the backs of her eyes.

Eleanor picked up her reticule and dipped a slightly rigid curtsy. "Goodbye, Andrew. I—I am deeply indebted to you for making my Season so successful and—and goodbye!"

She gathered together every ounce of dignity she possessed and swept past Andrew into the hallway, deeply aware that he made not the slightest move to stop her.

Chapter Nineteen

Eleanor floated into the hallway with her head held high and what she hoped was a certain amount of dignity. She was burningly aware that Lady Glower, Iris, and a household of servants were watching her with wide, curious eyes, and doubled her efforts to appear as if her heart were not broken and her emotional balance seriously at risk.

For the benefit of the servants she bestowed upon both her aunt and her cousin a very calm and affectionate salute, saying, "How much I have enjoyed my stay here. I shall tell Papa of all your kindness to me, dear Aunt, and dear, dear Cousin! I shall miss you both, and you must promise to let me return the favor by visiting me very soon!"

Iris, her eyes shining bright with unshed tears and her expression tragic, clasped Eleanor's hands and gave them a meaningful squeeze. "Oh, Cousin! I beg you, please do not go! Not like this!"

"But my carriage is ready," said Eleanor, gently, "and there truly is nothing to dissuade me now."

Iris sobbed, and the tears spilled over as she watched Eleanor leave the house and step out into the bright morning sunshine.

The last of her trunks were being strapped into place and, as she waited for this task to be accomplished, she could not prevent herself from looking back at Glower House one last time.

There, standing on the top step, was Andrew, looking very much like the devil himself with his black cloak swirling about him in the soft morning breeze and his expression dark and unwavering.

In that look Eleanor read censure, and not the least trace of tenderness or affection. It was a hard lesson to learn that she had fallen in love with a man who could be so coldhearted as to look upon her with such a wrathful expression, but she told herself she was quite glad to have learned it now instead of later.

A footman sprang forward to open the carriage door and let down the steps. He held out his arm expectantly, ready to assist Eleanor into the carriage. There was now nothing for it but to board the chaise and return home, to live out the rest of her days as a cronish spinster, as she had once promised Iris she would, and forget that she had ever lost her heart to a man who was so apparently unfeeling that he could silently watch her leave without the least show of emotion or regret.

It would never do, resolved Eleanor, for Andrew to see just how disappointed and hurt she was. She schooled her expression to one of impassivity, and she raised her chin one defiant notch as she set her small, gloved hand on the footman's arm. She hoped Andrew would finally realize that she did indeed intend to leave and that he would be overcome by such despair that he would at last beg her not to go.

But Andrew was looking far from desolate. Instead, he smiled suddenly—a confident, determined smile that held more purpose than humor.

He had seen Eleanor's chin jut to a defiant angle, and he knew very well from experience that whenever she struck such a pose, it was to prevent her wounds being touched.

So she wasn't as unfeeling as she was trying to make him believe! He was down the steps and across the walk before Eleanor could realize it.

He dismissed the footman with a glance and directed a piercing gaze at her. "I shall assist Lady Eleanor into the carriage myself. That is, if that is what she *wants* me to do."

Eleanor suddenly found her hand in Andrew's strong grasp. "Of course! I mean—nothing has happened that may induce me to stay," she said, in an oddly fluttering voice.

"Far be it from me to try to influence your decision," said Andrew, with perfect calm, "but it occurs to me that you are about to leave London without being made aware of certain information."

"What—what information do you mean?"

"That I am not as peacock-proud as you would have the world believe. I see a doubt in your eyes. Shall I prove it?"

Eleanor was too confused by this admission to answer. A grave mistake, for Andrew mistook her silence for assent and, still holding her hand, he dropped down on one knee before her.

She gasped and found her voice, although it was considerably weakened. "What—what *are* you doing?"

"Acting incautiously without consideration for what people may think."

Eleanor recognized her own words coming back to her, but she also recognized the astonished faces of her aunt and cousin, who were staring stock-still from the top of the front steps. "Andrew! You—you cannot do this!"

"No? Then may I tell you how much I regret that wretched wager? May I tell you that never in the world would I deliberately hurt you?"

"Oh, *do* get up!" Eleanor tugged at her hand, still held firmly in his, and looked around frantically. She saw only her aunt's shocked countenance and the knowingly amused faces of the servants who stood crowded in the doorway behind their mistress. "Oh, *pray* stop at once, you absurd man! Heavens, I am *certain* that is Lord Montfort driving towards us! What shall he think?"

"I don't intend to tease myself over anything that interests me so little!"

"Then you might have a care for what he shall think of *me!* Gracious, it *is* Lord Montfort! Oh, *please* get up! If you are doing this merely to get even with me, to prove that you are not arrogant after all, I beg you will not!"

"Well, I'm not doing it for my own benefit, for it's curst uncomfortable down here."

"Then do get up!"

"Willingly. As soon as I have your assurance that you will marry me."

Eleanor went very still. "Marry you?"

"Monfort is almost upon us. Say, yes, Eleanor."

She looked up and saw that his lordship had indeed tooled his phaeton within ogling distance of the picture they presented on the front walk of Grosvenor Square. She was half tempted to succumb to Andrew and give him the answer he wanted, but some impulse prevented her doing so. Instead, she gripped his fingers, still holding hers, convulsively, and fixed him with a penetrating stare. "*Why* do you want to marry me?"

He smiled slightly. So, the little baggage wanted to wring every drop of blood out of him, did she? Well, she was to have it. "Because, you vengeful little hoyden, I have discovered that I cannot live without you. I have also discovered that having tasted the sweetness of your kisses but once, I have developed an unconscionable addiction for them. I want to kiss you again and again, and I shan't be able to so unless you are with me always."

He felt her small hand tremble in his just before he saw the dazzling smile of happiness transform her face.

"Yes," she said, quite simply. "Oh, yes, Andrew!"

He was on his feet and had his strong arms about her in one swift and graceful movement. Then, lest she harbor any doubts about his admitted addiction, he kissed her quite thoroughly and rather ruthlessly.

Eleanor came to her senses with an effort. "Oh! Lord Montfort has just driven by and has seen our shocking conduct, I am sure of it!"

"He is welcome to it. With his penchant for gossip, he shall very shortly have it all over town that I am so sunk in depravity that I was kissing you on the street, and I shall be saved the trouble of posting the banns."

Eleanor frowned with a sudden thought. "You must stop him from spreading such tattle, Andrew! Everyone shall think you were kissing me to win the wager, and no one shall believe you kissed me merely because you wanted to!''

"Good God, Eleanor, shall you never let me forget that blasted bet?''

"No,'' she retorted, bluntly. "Nor will I allow you to forget that you once called me that horrid, hateful name!''

He looked down at her, a curious light in his dark eyes and a smile teasing the fine line of his lips. "You mean Lady Chill? *That* was indeed a mistake. Having held you in my arms, I am well aware that there is nothing chilly at all about you!''

She tried to look severe but blushed rosily. "Andrew! You—you cannot say such things, you *sinful* creature!''

He laughed softly at her confusion. Then, lest she decide to take him to task for any other of his iniquities, he scooped her up in his arms, kissed her soundly yet again, and carried her back up the steps and into Glower House.

IF ROMANCE BE THE FRUIT OF LIFE—
READ ON—
BREATH-QUICKENING HISTORICALS FROM PINNACLE

WILDCAT (722, $4.99)
by Rochelle Wayne

No man alive could break Diana Preston's fiery spirit . . . until seductive Vince Gannon galloped onto Diana's sprawling family ranch. Vince, a man with dark secrets, would sweep her into his world of danger and desire. And Diana couldn't deny the powerful yearnings that branded her as his own, for all time!

THE HIGHWAY MAN (765, $4.50)
by Nadine Crenshaw

When a trumped-up murder charge forced beautiful Jane Fitzpatrick to flee her home, she was found and sheltered by the highwayman—a man as dark and dangerous as the secrets that haunted him. As their hiding place became a place of shared dreams—and soaring desires—Jane knew she'd found the love she'd been yearning for!

SILKEN SPURS (756, $4.99)
by Jane Archer

Beautiful Harmony Harper, leader of a notorious outlaw gang, rode the desert plains of New Mexico in search of justice and vengeance. Now she has captured powerful and privileged Thor Clarke-Jargon, who is everything Harmony has ever hated—and all she will ever want. And after Harmony has taken the handsome adventurer hostage, she herself has become a captive—of her own desires!

WYOMING ECSTASY (740, $4.50)
by Gina Robins

Feisty criminal investigator, July MacKenzie, solicits the partnership of the legendary half-breed gunslinger-detective Nacona Blue. After being turned down, July—never one to accept the meaning of the word no—finds a way to convince Nacona to be her partner . . . first in business—then in passion. Across the wilds of Wyoming, and always one step ahead of trouble, July surrenders to passion's searing demands!

FOR THE VERY BEST IN ROMANCE—
DENISE LITTLE PRESENTS!

AMBER, SING SOFTLY (0038, $4.99)
by Joan Elliott Pickart

Astonished to find a wounded gun-slinger on her doorstep, Amber Prescott can't decide whether to take him in or put him out of his misery. Since this lonely frontierswoman can't deny her longing to have a man of her own, she nurses him back to health, while savoring the glorious possibilities of the situation. But what Amber doesn't realize is that this strong, handsome man is full of surprises!

A DEEPER MAGIC (0039, $4.99)
by Jillian Hunter

From the moment wealthy Margaret Rose and struggling physician Ian MacNeill meet, they are swept away in an adventure that takes them from the haunted land of Aberdeen to a primitive, faraway island—and into a world of danger and irresistible desire. Amid the clash of ancient magic and new science Margaret and Ian find themselves falling helplessly in love.

SWEET AMY JANE (0050, $4.99)
by Anna Eberhardt

Her horoscope warned her she'd be dealing with the wrong sort of man. And private eye Amy Jane Chadwick was used to dealing with the wrong kind of man, due to her profession. But nothing prepared her for the gorgeously handsome Max, a former professional athlete who is being stalked by an obsessive fan. And from the moment they meet, sparks fly and danger follows!

MORE THAN MAGIC (0049, $4.99)
by Olga Bicos

This classic romance is a thrilling tale of two adventurers who set out for the wilds of the Arizona territory in the year 1878. Seeking treasure, an archaeologist and an astronomer find the greatest prize of all—love.